No Odes to Widows

No Odes to Widows

by Kay Taylor Burnett

iUniverse, Inc.

New York   Bloomington

No Odes to Widows

This is a work of fiction. All of the characters, names, incidents, organizations, and dialogue in this novel are either the products of the author's imagination or are used fictitiously.

iUniverse books may be ordered through booksellers or by contacting:

iUniverse
1663 Liberty Drive
Bloomington, IN 47403
www.iuniverse.com
1-800-Authors (1-800-288-4677)

Because of the dynamic nature of the Internet, any Web addresses or links contained in this book may have changed since publication and may no longer be valid. The views expressed in this work are solely those of the author and do not necessarily reflect the views of the publisher, and the publisher hereby disclaims any responsibility for them.

ISBN: 978-1-4401-3597-2 (sc)
ISBN: 978-1-4401-3599-6 (dj)
ISBN: 978-1-4401-3598-9 (ebook)

Printed in the United States of America

iUniverse rev. date: 4/16/2009

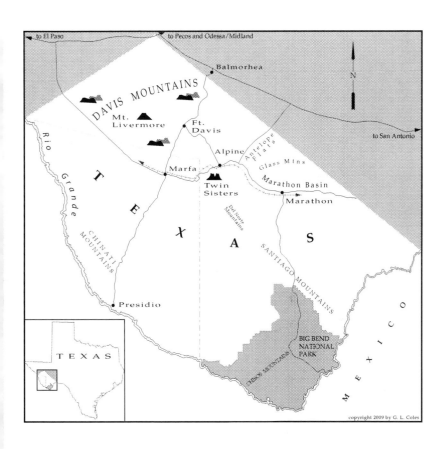

My gratitude to Alice Stevens for the front cover photograph, and to Gail Rider, Stacie Legge, Sandra Scofield, Tom Shuford, John Taylor, Steve Floch, Anne Frye, and the Marfa Writer's Group, who took the time to listen and to encourage my writing this first novel.

This book is dedicated to Eve Trook, Julia Maverick, Doris Sipes, Dodie Meeks, Peggy Coston, and to widows everywhere whose stories have not been heard.

"My tale was heard and yet it was not told."
Chidiock Tichborne, 1558–1586
(Written the night before he was hanged in the Tower of London.)

CHAPTER ONE

The old wooden pier jutted into Galveston Bay from the lawn of a cypress, two-story house. Three figures lay across the pier, skimming their fingers into the salt water at tiny, darting fish. The sun was warm on their backs as they laughed—the curly-haired child on one side, the love of her life on the other with his arm stretched over them both ...

Headlights burst upon Katherine's reverie. A small car swept past her on a highway curve, narrowly missing her rear fender as it careened toward an oncoming vehicle.

"Idiot!" she screamed, straining to wrench her SUV off the rain-slicked road. She skidded to a stop on the muddy easement, jolting her companion from the passenger seat to the floorboard with a thud.

All grew quiet again. The road was pitch black ahead and behind.

"Bananas?" she whispered in the dark. "Are you all right?"

The little spaniel climbed up on the seat and into Katherine's lap.

"That was close," she said, hugging the puppy and smoothing its trembling ears. "Too close."

Far West Texas was known for its clear starry nights. This was not one of them. Katherine felt hemmed in by the darkness beyond the rain-drizzled windows in the hours before dawn. But thankfully, her long drive from Houston to Alpine was almost over.

She'd gone to the big city to settle her husband's estate and had intended to stay a while. She drove instead of flying Southwest Airlines so she could take Bananas with her. She spent her first day in Houston looking at condominiums—which was exciting at first—but she'd fled the following day, overwhelmed by the crush of city noise and traffic and distraught after meeting with the nest of bankers and lawyers. The ten-hour drive was finally near the end.

A bolt of white flashed from the center of heaven and connected to a distant peak of the Davis Mountains. A jarring crescendo followed, and hard rain turned to icy sleet.

Katherine shuddered and pulled Bananas close again. "I wish we were home."

Her arms fell to her lap, and she rested her head against the seat. "Home?" she sighed. "Brann was home, no matter where we lived or where we were."

Her fingers fluffed the little dog's ears. "Now it's just you and me."

Bananas licked Katherine's wet cheeks before being gently nudged back into the passenger seat.

Katherine continued her drive into Alpine.

* * *

Sam Bassinger drove fast and west out of the Marathon Basin on the same route he'd taken earlier that morning. He kept one hand on the steering wheel, lifted a cell phone from his shirt pocket, and punched a name displayed on its panel.

"Hey, I'm headin' to Alpine to make contact for those deliveries. Where you gonna be?"

"I'm goin' to Alpine too. Havin' breakfast at Yummy Chow," a deep voice responded.

"See you there." Sam snapped the phone shut.

He viewed his image in the rearview mirror, adjusting his perfectly creased Western hat and smoothing his mustache and goatee. He smiled and winked at his own reflection. "Hey, good lookin'."

Staring down the long, straight highway, he saw cars clustered less than a mile ahead. Uniformed men were herding them into a single lane a few at a time from both directions. A dozen law enforcement cars were parked on the right side of the highway while officers scurried around yellow plastic ribbon marked CRIME SCENE. He slowed near a deputy sheriff standing in the westbound lane motioning vehicles left.

"What the hell?" Sam squeezed his eyes into focus out the window, leaning across the bulk of a big boxer puppy asleep on the seat. "Now whaddaya think's goin' on?"

The dog raised his head as Sam peered out the window and swiped his tongue across Sam's face.

"Not now, Rasputin!"

Sam vigorously rubbed his wet jaw on his coat sleeve and craned his neck again at the yellow chalk outline of a human figure on the roadside.

"Mother of God!" he rasped. "I hope they're not stopping every car!"

Glancing back at his pickup bed, he saw no trace of recent cargo and released a tight huff of air. He rummaged in his shirt pocket for cigarettes, keeping one hand on the wheel to navigate the single-file traffic moving west. He pulled one from the pack, dropped it in his lap, and scrambled to retrieve it.

His hand shook as he punched the lighter into the dashboard. When it popped red and glowing, he lit the cigarette with a deep draw and opened the truck window a few inches. He checked his image again in the side mirror and watched himself spew smoke from the side of his mouth into the icy cold morning.

A final deputy waved him through the end of the bottleneck, and Sam held his course past the Y at Antelope Flats, releasing his breath in a blast.

The mountains began to ease back from the roadway into sloping grasslands drenched with rain. Across the grassy savannahs to the north, the purple point of Miter Peak rose from the Davis Mountain range. Sam drove straight ahead toward the Twin Sisters, which were skirted in clouds, their peaks poking high above Alpine.

Ten minutes later he was in town passing Sul Ross State University on his right. The red brick, Ivy League buildings from the late 1800s looked surreal on the side of a prickly-pear–studded mountain, as if they'd been lifted from an East Coast campus and plopped like props on a stage.

He slowed near the highway fork, where a blinking red light signaled the start of one-way traffic west. A familiar face smiled from the sidewalk, as a bare hand popped out to wave from beneath a red cape and lavender scarf flapping in the wind.

Sam gritted his teeth. "Professor Kemp!"

That woman turns up at every environmental hearing in one of those outlandish costumes, leading the charge to protect every last blade of grass and obscure creature ever known in Texas.

He forced a grin and tooted his horn, wondering how she'd react if she knew he was on the other side of that political fence. Chuckling out loud, he imagined himself outrunning a fat lady with a limp, thrashing her cane about.

Sam drove toward a small mom-and-pop café wedged in the midst of a hodgepodge of little shops lining the north side of Holland Avenue. He scanned the opposite side of the street that bordered the potholed parking lot of a rundown train depot. The rumble of a freight train beat clickity-clack, clickity-clack through downtown, and he nearly sprang through the windshield when the whistle screamed. Rasputin whined and laid his head across Sam's lap.

"How do you think these folks deal with fifteen trains running through town every day, Pute? It must scramble the eggs in their cartons." He scratched the boxer's ears. "You're mighty good company, pal. Always listening, never talking back."

Rasputin's eyes glistened as he bounced up and pressed his considerable bulk into Sam's ribs. The dog yawned with a loud whine and sprawled back across the bright Mexican blanket on the seat to lay his head in a slant of early October sunlight.

Sam spotted a parking space in front of the dry goods store and aimed his truck into the space, cut the engine, and cracked the passenger window an inch.

"OK, buddy. I'll bring home the bacon! You stay put."

Rasputin knew the word *bacon*. He sat up, twitching his tail and quickening his pants as his tongue lolled from his mouth.

Sam stretched his long legs onto the sidewalk, tucking a crisp shirttail into razor-creased jeans. He didn't lock the doors. Crime, like parking, wasn't a problem in a town of eight thousand five hundred residents—counting every last student at Sul Ross. At least crime wasn't a problem for him.

Bells clanged as Sam pushed through the front door of Yummy Chow and headed toward the cash register.

"Mornin'. I'll take black coffee, eggs over easy, extra bacon, and some of Billie's toasted bread."

"You got it!" The café owner smiled and adjusted a Red Sox baseball cap over a graying ponytail. He turned to the big, metal coffee urn, poured steaming dark brew to the brim of a white mug, and swung it onto the counter. "They say we could get snow."

Sam looked swiftly around the room and back with a stiff shrug. "Yeah."

Thumbing through some bills pulled from his jeans pocket, he peeled off a few and laid the money on the counter. His nerves were still jangled from the highway scene, causing his hand to wobble as he picked up the heavy mug of coffee. The hot liquid slopped over the side. He grunted and crossed the crowded room, looking around.

His eyes rested on a neatly groomed couple sitting near the café's front windows. Sauntering that direction, he paused and tipped his hat as he made eye contact with the woman. A flash of dislike crossed her face, and he quickly averted his eyes as he took a seat at an empty table behind her.

Barrett Compton leaned around his wife and looked with a puzzled expression at Sam seated apart from them. He motioned Sam over.

"Later," Sam mouthed.

Amid low murmuring in the dining area, a telephone rang. A slender, college-age waitress nosily shifted a stack of dirty dishes from her arms to a nearby plastic bin and grabbed the phone from the wall behind the cash register.

"Yummy Chow Café! Can I he'p ya?"

Sam stared at her firm, round rump and leaned back, smiling as an older waitress slid a steaming breakfast in front of him.

"Thanks," he acknowledged.

As he unwrapped the utensils rolled in a paper napkin, his eyes returned to the pleasant distraction. The young waitress now held the phone at her side, looking wide-eyed and slack-jawed, as she shook her head.

Sam began sopping up his eggs with a thick slice of toast. He was well versed about women and their reactions when dumped and could never understand all that wasted emotion.

"Frank Johnson's been shot!" the waitress screeched.

Sam's head shot up, and his eyes met Barrett's. Dishes stopped clattering, voices ceased chattering, and the room fell pin-drop silent.

"They, they found his body by the side of the road, jest this side of Marathon, 'bout dawn this mornin'." She held the phone in one hand while the other squeezed the corners of a white apron tied at her waist. Her face was furrowed in a look of disbelief.

"They say he'd been investigatin' an eighteen-wheeler."

Sam glared again at Barrett Compton, who was as white as a sheet, his Adam's apple bobbing in his skinny throat. Sam shook his head, placing a finger to his lips.

A burst of voices ripped through the silence as everyone began talking at once.

Barrett and his wife pushed up from their seats and headed to the door. He nodded curtly at Sam in passing.

* * *

Highway Patrol Captain Bill Butler stood at the door of a small frame house and knocked. He bit into his dry, chapped lips and smoothed a trickle of blood with his tongue.

"Just a minute," a cheery voice sang from within. "I'm coming."

Trudy Johnson pulled the front door back and stood barefoot in the doorway wearing a snug red T-shirt and jeans. Long blond hair tumbled around her pretty face.

"Why, Captain Butler," she said with a smile. "What brings you here?" She swept a stray curl back from her forehead.

For a moment Butler held her soft blue eyes with his own, steeled and ready. He lowered his head and looked up again at her eyes grown wide as saucers, her frozen smile revealing even, white teeth.

"Where's my husband?"

"I'm sorry, Ms. Johnson ..."

"Not Frank," she whispered. "Not Frank!" she screamed and slumped against the doorframe.

Butler placed a firm hand on the woman's small upper arms to keep her from sagging to the ground.

"Mommy?" a high voice called from inside the house.

"I'll help you inside, Ms. Johnson," Butler said quietly. He held her firmly and half carried her into the front room.

A little boy came running, tiny boots drumming the floor. He wrapped his arms around his mother's leg and peeked up at the officer.

Butler glanced around. The living room was minimally furnished. A cheap, beige sofa, a matching chair, and a small, glass-top coffee table sat at a distance from the vinyl recliner that he guessed was Frank's. A large television was across from it.

He led the woman to the sofa and slowly sat down with her. The toddler clung to his mother's leg as she sobbed, her head falling against Butler's chest.

Butler breathed deeply; she smelled like freshly mown grass of summer. One hand patted her soft shoulder while he extended the other firmly to the little boy's head. Looking around, he noticed worn but spotlessly clean linoleum floors. Photographs in gold-tinted frames sat on the television and hung high on the wall behind the sofa: Frank beside his Texas Highway Patrol car; Trudy in her wedding gown with Frank in his uniform as they cut their wedding cake; numerous pictures of a baby with a progression of one-, two-, and three-year-old birthday photos; parents; grandparents.

"May I call someone to come stay with you?" he asked gently.

No response.

He waited.

"Ms. Johnson, is there someone you'd like me to call?"

The young woman's head stayed buried in his chest.

The child looked up at Butler. "You can call my daddy."

Butler smoothed the boy's hair before reaching inside a coat pocket for his cell phone.

"Butler here. Schedule two officers to stay two-hour shifts with Ms. Johnson today. Get them here as quick as possible."

* * *

Butler drove slowly from the Johnson house to his headquarters on Sul Ross Avenue. Breaking the bad news to a fellow officer's family was the toughest part of command.

He relived the scene from the wee hours earlier that morning ... when he had been crouched in darkness over a body sprawled face down on the shoulder of the blacktop west of Marathon ...

Early winter winds had driven rain from Mexico into high mountain crevices and covered the desert flatlands with an icy blanket of drizzle and fog. It was cold, and so was the corpse at his feet.

This was new territory, his first command in the Big Bend Trans Pecos region and his first encounter with homicide in the margins of Far West Texas.

On one hand he felt relief. He was out of that mind-strangling desk job in Austin, which he had endured for his daughter's sake. When she left for college, he had landed this job on the last frontier in Texas.

On the other hand, he was looking at a dead colleague.

Butler flicked his eyes upward at the sound of approaching footsteps. He stood tall, snapping to attention as a wall of a man strode toward him in the glare of makeshift lights. He searched the face of Ambrose Trent, a Texas Ranger known to him only by newspaper photographs and legend.

Butler knew the importance of first impressions, and a good one was necessary if he was to garner the respect and cooperation necessary for command. This could be his last tour of duty before retirement, and he planned to maintain a legacy of excellence.

Eye to eye with the ranger, he raised two fingers to his Stetson brim. "Captain Butler here, sir. The area's been secured. The sheriff should be here any minute."

"Good," the ranger said. "And daylight can't come too soon."

The scene, with hazy halogen lights and shadows in the fog, felt bizarre to Butler, more like an old-time whodunit movie. He shook the feeling and studied the ranger's face. It looked worn by the elements, like the volcanic terrain of the parched borderlands that he was just getting to know.

Deep barrel tones echoed in the desert air as the ranger spoke. "Seems that Johnson was in the wrong place at the wrong time."

Butler watched Ranger Trent reach beneath his rain poncho and down vest, pull a cigar from an inner pocket, and strip the wrapper with long, thin fingers, freckled and dry.

"It could happen to any one of us, anywhere, anytime," Trent conceded, lowering his voice to a rumble.

He bit off the end of the cigar, spit, and hunched his back to the wind and drizzle. His rain-splattered Western hat covered short bristles of gray hair, its brim sheltering the tobacco roll in his teeth. He yanked a lighter from somewhere beneath the poncho, and with a flick of his thumb, a flame burst beneath the cigar. He inhaled deeply and languidly blew smoke.

Butler caught a whiff of the pungent aroma in the wind. A flapping sound startled him, and he peered cautiously at the Texas Highway Patrol officers in their billowing rain slickers who had arrived on the scene shortly after he had. Light was beginning to filter through the darkness. He searched the highway for any sign of the Brewster County sheriff's arrival. This was the sheriff's jurisdiction, and Butler didn't plan on any petty one-upmanship regarding rank or authority.

His attention came back to the ranger. He could tell by the firm set of Trent's jaw that the lawman understood the low-level terror involved in working alone day and night, patrolling miles of open country where criminals of all kinds plied their trade.

"I'm new out here, but I'll do everything I can to help you and the sheriff find this killer." Butler's words formed small, white clouds of warm air in the gray chill.

He unzipped his jacket a few inches with fingers mottled blue with cold and lifted a paper from inside. "This is for you."

He passed the folded paper to Trent. "It's the documentation of the last call Officer Johnson made as to his location and the license number of an eighteen-wheeler rig he was checking."

Trent reached out and fumbled the paper; Butler shot an arm forward, snatching the sheet before it fluttered to the wet ground.

He held the paper out to Trent again. "When Johnson didn't call back within thirty minutes, I was notified, and a local alert went out to find him."

Trent held the report with knotty, stiff fingers. "Let me get my goggles."

He winced and retrieved a pair of wire-rimmed glasses from an inner coat pocket and shook the document open. "It's hell gettin' old."

He fitted the readers over the bridge of his long, straight nose, tilted his head back, and flashed his green eyes across the page.

Butler heard him heave a sigh as he slowly refolded the paper and slipped it into a hip pocket.

Trent removed the glasses, and his voice seethed through teeth clenched around the cigar. "We'll catch the son of a bitch."

Butler felt the ranger sizing him up through squinted eyes, sharp and clear. He involuntarily tightened his fists with determination. He knew he was one of the best in criminal investigations, and he wanted the ranger to know it too. He kept his gaze steady on Trent, who casually puffed the cigar, lifting his chin to expel clouds of curling smoke.

"Tell me what you saw when you got here," the ranger commanded.

"Yes, sir." Butler fixed on the memory of the young, clean-cut officer on the ground, bloody and still.

"It was about 4:00 AM. Dark. Wet. Cold drizzle, and sleet. Silent."

He shivered and hoped the ranger would think his reaction was due to the icy morning. He'd been nineteen when his short stint in Vietnam ended, dispelling youthful naiveté forever—but never the revulsion of death.

"No sound except Johnson's radio. It was on, sir. His headlights too, barely visible in the fog." Butler shunted his face down and kicked a clod of dirt with the toe of his boot, angry that he'd had no time to personally train the young officer in border warfare beyond the basics.

He met Trent's eyes again. "It was execution style, sir. Shot in the back of the head at close range. Small entry wound. Could be something like a nine-millimeter semiautomatic."

He paused and thought of how many guns were out there of that make. *Millions.*

"The projectile blew the left side of his face away." He stood still, the scene reminiscent of his time in Nam. He shifted his eyes toward the victim's empty patrol car with the familiar freeze of feelings.

"The body was cold and soaking wet, but rigor mortis hadn't set in when I got here."

Ranger Trent dipped his head toward the patrol car's gaping doors. "Was his video camera on?"

Butler sucked his breath and turned his collar up over his ears. "We may never know. The bastards pried it from the center console and took it with them."

17

Trent blew cigar smoke with a noisy snort, his frustration evident and understood by Butler.

Together they turned and looked at the fresh chalk outline beneath the newly erected tent.

Butler stared as the constant drizzle formed rivulets on the ground, draining definition. He thought how transitory life was, what we are and what we do ebbing away with time.

He glanced up at the white ambulance parked nearby—stark in the growing gray light—ready to encase the shell of a man. *The final patrol.*

Popping lights brought his attention back to the forensic crews and photographers flashing shutters at every inch of ground where the young patrolman had lain in a pool of his own blood. A number of officers were on their knees sifting for clues.

Butler brooded over their presence. When a lawman died in the line of duty, everyone turned out—even those off duty, on vacation, in retirement, or from neighboring towns in this sparsely settled twenty-two thousand square miles of badlands north of the Rio Grande, the river that divides Mexico and the United States.

Trent dropped the dwindling cigar stub to the ground and mashed it with the toe of his boot. "Anything missin' besides that camera?"

Butler jerked to attention again. "His gun, sir." He stiffened his lips and glared at the chalk outline. *A gun didn't make a man invincible.* "The key to the media box was in his pocket. So was his wallet."

The ranger's eyes looked distant, his face drawn as he pulled a fresh cigar from his shirt pocket and removed the clear cellophane wrapper.

Butler's stomach churned, as it had since he got the call. The ranger's slow, deliberate actions set him on edge.

Justice is never swift.

He searched his own pockets for a roll of Tums to soothe the acid rising in his throat and nearly gagged on the dry, chalky mint.

"That audio-visual equipment is vital. Shoulda been mighty conspicuous," Trent grunted as he drew hard to ignite the new smoke, "carryin' that heavy, little box in plain sight of the highway."

Butler clenched his jaw. *Somebody knew what they were doing, destroying that evidence.* Johnson had been his man, his responsibility, a fine young officer fresh out of training with a wife and child.

He watched the older lawman snuff the fresh cigar and lift the yellow crime tape. Trent stood in his monogrammed stovepipe boots—"A. T." appliquéd in white on black—beside the eighteen-wheeler tracks etched lightly in mushy, wet limestone.

"I see you're gettin' prints," Ranger Trent called to a forensic officer dusting the car.

Butler glanced over at the officer Trent had addressed. He was familiar; a veteran with whom he'd worked near Austin. The man responded with a nod at the ranger and looked over toward Butler, raising his thumb in recognition.

Butler considered the challenge of moisture in the dusting process. Smudging was inevitable. Dumb luck might provide one clear print. But he'd always said he'd rather be lucky than rich.

His eyes followed Trent as he ventured beyond the marked-off area near the highway. Butler saw him stop near the soggy fence line, kneel, and take a ballpoint pen from an inside pocket. He used it to prod an item nestled in a clump of native grass.

"Hey, Butler." The ranger turned his face up to catch Butler's eye. "Put this here in one of those evidence bags."

Butler flushed. *Damn it! How could our team have missed that?*

He nodded to a young patrolman who plucked the cigarette butt from the ground with a rubber-gloved hand and placed it in a brown paper bag.

"Seems we got a smoker who hand-rolls," the ranger drawled.

"Is it Mexican or U.S.?"

"The tobacco? Good question," the ranger acknowledged.

Butler spun around, pacing back to the highway to recheck the soaked ground and make additional notes for his files. Once again he noted the tire marks of a pickup truck, heavy when it pulled over, light when it left. Another set of narrow tracks was wedged into the semi-wet muck in front of the patrol car.

He knew the rules of procedure; it was the sheriff who would make a call for casting. He also knew that the ranger outranked them all.

"Let's get some photos and casts of these tire treads!" he yelled, and then added grudgingly, "As soon as the sheriff gets here."

"Get those casts now!" the ranger bellowed. "Before the rain washes 'em away!"

Butler felt relief—he had gotten what he wanted. But he fretted; *he must think I'm an idiot!*

"Right!" he shouted back with a deadpan expression as he waved the forensic team over. He pulled the Tums again from his pocket and pried two from the open roll.

Light came seeping through the fog; time was slipping away. He looked westward as headlights reared upon the horizon and watched a convoy of vehicles with flashing red lights swallow the highway through yellow grassland and the blue ranges of Del Norte and the Glass Mountains. The dreamlike vista mesmerized until the green and white sheriff's cars pulled to a halt near the ambulance that now held a lifeless man in uniform.

Butler trudged toward the sheriff with a second copy of his report in hand, silently vowing to use his hard-earned knowledge as a law enforcement officer to help find this killer and earn the sheriff and ranger's respect.

* * *

A short, plump woman continued briskly across the Sul Ross State University campus, red cape flapping, a hand-whittled staff strengthening her gait. She reached her office out of breath, flushed and damp with chilly mist.

A student sitting behind the desk sang out to her, "Good morning, Professor Kemp. You have an early meeting with Sandy Wisner this morning."

The professor cocked her head at her assistant. "Good morning?"

"I scheduled the meeting last week—about his thesis?" the student explained.

"Oh?" The professor looked thoughtful.

"I sent you an e-mail," her assistant defended.

"Right!" Doris Kemp removed her fogged spectacles and wiped the round lenses on her wool cape. Replacing the eyewear, she took a deep breath. "This may take until noon."

The young assistant shrugged.

The professor marched into her book-lined inner sanctum, removed the red mantle, draped it with her long purple scarf over the back of a swivel chair, and rummaged around the cluttered desk. She grasped a small calendar and raised her head at a light tap-tap.

In the doorway stood a thin, young man of medium height. Dark circles ringed shirking eyes, and a shock of blond hair fell across a boyish but somber face. This graduate student, as always, was precisely on time, carrying his file of thesis notes in a way that suggested he never had to search for anything.

The professor clicked her tongue and sank heavily into the padded chair behind her desk. She peered at Sandy Wisner over the top of the spectacles perched on her nose. "Come in."

Wisner walked directly to an empty chair on the opposite side of the professor's desk and slumped into it. "I'm not sure I want to continue in criminal justice," he muttered with an edge in his voice.

The professor searched the troubled face and arranged her own to hide a smile. She knew how to make Sandy Wisner laugh. "Poetry, perhaps?"

Wisner stood abruptly, turned his back on the professor, and walked out.

Doris sat stunned. *What's gotten into him?*

She checked the tiny timepiece that hung on a delicate chain around her neck and sighed. "Oh, well. Now I have all morning to work on my paper."

* * *

Katherine Bell carried a cup of coffee out to the back porch of her house. She inhaled, bracing her lungs with cold mountain air. A thick-coated, white dog with curly ears and tan markings stood close by.

The liquid sloshed when she jerked at the sudden, unexpected honk of wild geese drifting into the gray morning mist. She brushed the coffee from her jacket sleeve, pulled a chair from the table with another stiff breath, and sat down. The puppy lay at her feet.

The wet scent of purple sage and cedar soothed but didn't dispel the shroud of grief that clung to her. She pondered earlier events. She knew better than to drive ten hours straight from Houston last night, but the desire to get out of the city and return to the quiet, wide-open spaces of Far West Texas held sway. *Of course, I hadn't counted on a near collision ...*

She shivered and looked up, wrapping her arms around herself. Dark clouds merged over the Southwestern-style house that she and Brann had built and lived in for one fleeting year. It had been a year of his dying and her confusion.

"What I wouldn't give now for one moment in our big, soft bed, snuggled in his arms," she whispered to her canine friend.

She released her arms and pulled the collar of her jacket closer to her ears, peering through the splintered first light of morning. Buffalo and feather grass were bent with rain across her acre of land. The pleasant fragrance of burning piñon filled her senses as she watched smoke coiling from the chimney of a lone house above her on Hancock Hill.

Her eyes fastened on the house. She had spent enough hours sitting on her back porch to know the routine of these neighbors, and lately their pattern had become erratic.

"Something's wrong up there," she said and looked at Bananas. "Maybe I should call my brother—but he's always busy, too busy being a Texas Ranger for time with us."

She shrugged, set her coffee cup firmly on the table, and stood to stretch. "And this is no time for a pity party."

The dog jumped up on its back legs and pressed its front paws anxiously on Katherine's leg. Thunder cracked like a rifle shot, and rain mixed with ice pelted the porch.

Katherine knelt down and scooped Bananas into her arms. "It's all right. Don't be scared."

Straightening with the furry bundle, she jerked the dog closer at the sudden squeal of tires and spun around to see a dark green sports car skidding around the corner beyond her cedar post fence out back. It ripped along the back dirt road, spraying small rocks into the air and against the coyote fence.

Katherine stared and gasped. "I think that might be the car that nearly killed me last night!"

She watched the small car spiral up the mountainside and through the arched gateway of the solitary house with a red tiled roof.

* * *

"These salt-of-the-earth sons of bitches wrench my sphincter!" Susanna Perez raged. "If these folks continue to run too many cattle and goats on too little grass, even the savannahs will be nothing but sand in a few years!"

She stamped a clump of young sideoats into the soil of Mill-Ring Ranch outside Marfa, thankful that somebody cared enough about the planet and the problem of overgrazing to buy seed balls and grass starters from her nursery to replenish losses.

"Miss Pe-*rez*?" a hesitant, husky voice ventured. "It's 'bout noon. Might near dinnertime?"

Susanna turned to see Leroy Jones tip a dirty felt hat back on his balding head and wipe sweat from his brow with a faded red handkerchief despite the cold. She ignored his "dinnertime," knowing the country use of it meant lunch, but bristled at the pronunciation of her married name.

"It's pronounced *Par*-is, Leroy!"

She stopped, realizing that she was taking her frustrations out against a hundred years of tradition of Texans adding or subtracting misbegotten syllables to words. How could Leroy know the correct pronunciation for a Mexican name? He said it just the way everyone else did.

Susanna jerked a wide-brimmed straw hat from her head and pressed a shirtsleeve to her wet forehead.

"Sorry, Leroy. Let's break. I'm going to Alpine for lunch. I'll be back around three, or a little after. Can you come back startin' about one?"

"Yes, ma'am!" He nodded and shoved another clump of grass into the hole he had gouged with his trowel. With a few turns of the wrist, he mounded the sandy soil around it and knee-walked to the next spot.

How he could do it, Susanna didn't know. She worked in a squat, standing every few minutes to work the kinks out of her aching back and allow the blood rush to drain back from her tingling head. But Leroy could stay on his knees and punch holes all morning with those gnarled knuckles bulging from his old work gloves. He didn't seem to mind heat or the sun-baked ground, which could be as hard as granite.

She noticed that he'd settled back on his haunches to study the graying clouds. Susanna thought he looked worried as he placed an open hand on one knee and rose slowly, stamping dirt clumps from the soles of his battered boots.

"That is if it don't rain," he said.

She chuckled. Rain was about the only thing Leroy minded. The region was in the monsoon pattern where late summer and early autumn rains could easily wash away recent plantings.

Leroy gestured with a nod of leaving, and Susanna watched his bowlegged stroll toward the wide, metal gate and an ancient pickup truck.

She, too, worried about getting heavy rains before this job was finished. She needed that check to cover mounting bills. She squinted at the thunderheads forming to the west as she crossed the field opposite Leroy. She skimmed her tall, lean frame between two strands of barbed wire and approached a brand-new, double-cab pickup parked alongside the caliche road.

It was caliche, thank God, and not bentonite. Powdery bentonite, which was found along some unpaved roadways in Far West Texas, was dangerous. It clumped like kitty litter on the tires when wet, building girth until the tires couldn't roll. And "rolling them tires" was essential today to meet her friends for lunch, and maybe more so in getting to the nursery for that new order of plants.

After peeling off and tossing her work gloves and dirty boots into the truck bed, she hoisted herself up and onto the leather seat in the cab. Slinging her hat onto the seat, she eased her stocking feet into soft elk-skin, Western boots she had left on the floorboard before daylight that morning. Her satisfied smile reflected in the rearview mirror as she surveyed the fields where grass reclamation was beginning to show results.

She checked her wristwatch. The drive from Marfa to Alpine took just under thirty minutes, but the added fifteen miles from this outlying ranch meant she'd be haulin' to make the luncheon date with her friends, Katherine and Doris. Spending time with them was better than a trip to a shrink specializing in grief recovery.

What unlikely friends.

The adage "politics makes for strange bedfellows" popped into her mind.

Well, so does widowhood.

She'd met these women by chance one Saturday morning not long ago. They began talking as they waited in line at the Sixth Street Bakery & Café in Alpine to pick up fresh bread. They had little in common but for the biggie—widowhood.

Doris was middle-aged and had been living in town for a good number of years. She taught criminal justice at the university. Katherine was younger, a relative newcomer, and practically a recluse.

And here I am, Susanna Perez, a widow with two young'uns to raise.

She kept her eyes on the road and shut her mind to flashes of the car wreck that took the life of her husband and the father of her children. Instead, she shifted her thoughts to worries that it *might* rain and then Leroy might *not* return for the afternoon. She considered going back and finishing the job herself as she scanned the skies. She needed the money, but she also needed to be in town to meet Sam Bassinger about native plants.

So she went forward, just as she had since her husband died.

A small "Reduce Speed" sign outside Alpine's city limits reminded her of last week when Texas Highway Patrolman Frank Johnson had stopped her for speeding. She tapped the brake lightly.

Frank was so courteous when he leaned toward my car window. "Hello, Mrs. Perez. How are the kids?"

He'd given her a warning ticket then, but he might not again. Her carefully managed budget couldn't handle a cash outlay for a traffic fine. Christmas would be here before she knew it, and she needed extra income to juggle that. Maybe she should call about substitute teaching. But for now she needed to get to the café for lunch.

As Susanna drove into Alpine, she saw people standing on the sidewalks in small huddles. She frowned. Gatherings were unusual except for parades or town festivals. Most people were at their jobs.

Was it a holiday? That's when they gathered on the streets.

There was nothing going on in early October that she could recall.

She found a space and parked her truck around the corner from the café. She pulled a shoulder bag from beneath the seat and began striding to Sixth Street, reaching up to loosen a hair clasp that released long, reddish brown strands to stream behind her in the breeze.

As she walked through the doorway of the café, Alice Parsons, an older, pudgy woman with hair standing in blond coils, flowed out in layer upon layer of multicolored clothing.

"Did you hear about Frank Johnson being shot?" Alice screeched.

"Shot?" Susanna's jaw dropped. "Is he OK?"

"He's dead!"

"Dead?" Susanna stumbled backward, collided with the open door, and steadied herself as she shook her head. *Alice must be wrong.* She'd seen him just yesterday, waved to him as she picked her son up at school.

"No. He can't be."

"He is!" Alice declared. "Shot down like a dog out by the Marathon highway. And the cops don't know who did it." She shouldered Susanna aside to flounce away. "Gotta get to the post office and tell Millie."

"Oh my God," Susanna gasped. Her mouth stayed slightly open as she wandered toward the back of the dining area to an empty table where she slid onto a wooden chair.

The bells on the café door jangled. Susanna watched Doris pull the door open, backing against it to keep it from closing on Katherine who followed. Susanna rose from her chair to greet her friends but saw people tugging at Doris's red cape. The two women stopped beside a group clustered at the front of the café. Susanna heard Katherine gasp and watched as she turned around and squeezed passed Doris through the door. Doris rushed out of the café after her.

Susanna started to follow, and then halted and sank back into her seat knowing that she wasn't much good at comforting someone like Katherine. Her style was much too abrupt, and besides, she was too close to her own memories of loss and shock.

Her appetite gone, she went to the coffee bar and filled a cup, trying to pull herself together before meeting Sam Bassinger. Sam had sniffed after her even when she was a happily married woman. He seemed unfazed by her constant rejection.

Sam was handsome; she'd hand him that. And he had that attractive, little-boy-lost aura along with brains, brawn, and vanity. She knew he was the kind of man who took advantage of women, lavishing attention on at least a half dozen whom she knew of, letting them nurture him awhile before taking the next best offer that came along. She was lonely for male companionship, but heaven forbid. *Not Sam!*

* * *

Outside, fumbling in a coat pocket, Katherine sought the remote control gadget on her key ring and unlocked the SUV parked in front.

"Must get home," she mumbled and climbed in, her hands shaking as she groped for the seat belt buckle.

"Katherine!"

She stopped, turned a stony face to the passenger window, and saw Doris's crumpled brow peering through. Doris opened the passenger door and slid onto the passenger seat.

"Katherine." Doris's face was creased and taut. "I know that you're upset, but come on in and sit with me and Susanna."

Katherine closed her eyes and felt a touch on her shoulder.

"Do you want to talk?" Doris asked softly.

Katherine clenched her jaw as she poked the wrong key, twice, into the ignition. She gave up and dropped her hands in her lap.

"Death," she said in a low voice while staring straight ahead. "So *final*."

Her mind flew back to the year before her husband's death. Her beautiful and bright but troubled twenty-year-old daughter, Maureen, had jumped from an Austin rooftop.

Doris moved across the seat toward Katherine and gently touched her hand. Katherine hung her head and spoke almost in a whisper. "I was thinking of Maureen, off her medication, in a psychotic episode."

She raised her head and pressed it back against the seat, lapsing into memory. She pictured her husband, Brann, fragile with congestive heart problems, putting his arms around her at the hospital emergency room where Maureen had been taken, her own sobs shaking both bodies.

"Don't stop. Never stop," he'd said gently. She understood that he was giving her permission to weep and to go on weeping. Strangely, his words had been calming.

She felt a tear slide as she turned her head. *Was Doris saying something?*

"Katherine, listen to me. I know that you loved that child more than the next breath. But now! Now you are burying your very life with your husband."

Katherine saw the worry in her friend's face. "And why not?" she asked. "Everyone I love is gone."

"I know. It must be devastating," Doris said softly.

"I spent the final year of Brann's life in numbness over Maureen," Katherine spoke tonelessly. "My guilt at not being wholly there for him then consumes me now.

"Oh, Doris, I thought I was getting over it," she turned her eyes to Doris. "And just hearing of yet another death ..."

She could see her friend's distress and straightened her back against the seat. "I'm sorry, Doris, losing control like this."

Doris nodded and said matter-of-factly, "Sometimes the dam just has to leak so it don't break."

Katherine placed her hands on the steering wheel. "Doris, you need to go back inside. Susanna must be wondering what's going on." She brushed tears away. "I'm so sorry."

"Not to worry." Doris opened the car door and scooted out. She stood on the curb and leaned her head back into the vehicle.

"Do you want to come in?"

Katherine cast her eyes downward and shook her head.

"Shall I follow you home?"

"No, I'm fine. Bananas will be there." She forced a small laugh and met Doris's eyes. "I think that little dog is the reason I'm still alive."

"Call me this evening," Doris said firmly. "Maybe ..." She searched for words. "Maybe we can help find out who did this to the patrolman and his family. I have years of book learning on the subject. Finding out would help my career, help his family ..."

Katherine just stared.

Doris became more animated. "After all, we live in this community and hear things that law enforcement might never hear."

Katherine nodded.

"Like gossip," Doris continued, trying to bring Katherine around. "I have a lot of chatty resources. We can begin a clandestine investigation on our own."

"I need to go home for now," Katherine said, looking down.

Doris nodded and backed away from the vehicle, closing the door.

Katherine drove to her house and pulled her SUV into the back driveway. She saw a white tail waving like a flag at the gate.

Thank God for Bananas.

She thought of her brother, Ambrose, and wished they were closer.

* * *

Doris and Susanna sat together at the café, eating little of their soup-and-salad lunches. The place was filled with customers and hummed with hushed tones.

"You don't have to overhear them to know that they're talking about the murder," Susanna said.

Doris looked around the room, her eyes narrowing. "I can imagine a motive for murder in most every person here … but not of *Frank Johnson*.

"Death," she continued softly, turning back to Susanna, "death is still too close for Katherine." She peeped over her spectacles at Susanna's unusually pale face.

"I know." Susanna straightened her back and sat forward in her chair. "We *both* know."

"Death is the natural scheme of things," Doris soothed. "Not death by murder of course. And murder in a small town like ours is devastating. One would think that each of us would live every day as if it were our last. Widows know it better than most. Why don't we live that way?"

Susanna leaned over the table and spoke in a low voice. "Because most of us are just reacting to the past, Doris. Look at Katherine. She can't possibly connect with the outside world because she can't get out of that bubble she's in."

She slumped back in her chair. "I guess there must be a balance in knowing how fragile we are and living each day fully. I'll be danged if I know what it is."

Doris's eyes darted toward Alice Parsons, who had returned to wander around the café looking more lost than usual. "It's especially hard when you're left to face the ravages of old age. Alone." She sighed. "There are no odes to widows."

Susanna bobbed her head in agreement. "Just bad jokes."

She, too, turned to watch Alice for a moment and shuddered. "I hope that isn't *me* one day!"

"Trudy Johnson is now a widow," Doris interjected. "And despite our individuality, widows have much in common."

"I haven't met her," Susanna said, fishing in her purse.

"Trudy? She's lovely—with a lot of energy." Doris paused in reflection. "Poor Trudy. I know her from a fiber arts group."

Susanna checked the tab that the waitress had placed on their tabletop and took bills from her wallet. "So you've seen her—Trudy? Recently?"

"Actually, no. She normally attends on Thursday nights." Doris looked pensive. "That's when our weaving and fiber arts group meets. Come to think of it, the past few Thursdays Trudy has called to say she was sick and couldn't come." She lifted a small, round watch hanging from a gold chain around her neck and checked the time.

Susanna's chair scraped the floor, and Doris blurted, "I have some ideas about helping solve this crime. Do you want to help?"

Susanna stood up and stopped short, laughing. "You might as well ask Alice Parsons for all I know about sleuthing."

She stood behind her chair watching Doris's face. She sensed her friend's *need* to be involved, so she leaned forward and grinned. "But us Texas widder wimmen hafta stick together! Sure, I think we should put our heads together and help solve this murder. Just tell me what to do."

"Yes!" Doris exclaimed. "First," she raised one finger, "we need to go to the murder scene."

"Whoa! Tell me later. I gotta go." Susanna straightened and pushed the chair into the table. "I have a meeting with Sam Bassinger at two o'clock."

Doris's smile faded as she dropped her eyes to the table.

"Look, Doris," Susanna defended. "I don't have a job with a pension. And we both know that a pension is pivotal to a comfortable life. Sam has helped by supplying native plants to my nursery. Because of him I finally have the inventory to get the business of the new folks moving in and those from Austin coming out to buy and haul back. I couldn't make it without that extra business right now, much less later!"

Doris hesitated. "I hear you," she said. "But be careful. There's more than idle speculation as to which side of the fence Sam rides. That jury is still out."

* * *

Susanna heard a slight hum, like a whisper, and glanced up from her seat to see a Stetson hat suspended in midair, whirling in her office doorway.

Sam slipped from behind the doorjamb into the room, twirling the hat on his index finger.

"Miss Susanna." He smiled with a courtly bow.

"Have a seat." She nodded stiffly toward the chair next to her desk. Sam's never-ending advances annoyed the hell out of her.

She closed the screen of her laptop in a brisk, no-nonsense manner and sat erect in her chair. "Do you have more plants?"

"Yes, ma'am!" He leaned toward her.

She saw his eyes roam her body. It made her feel attractive—and then angry.

She remembered Doris's advice for caution. Selling contraband was a time-honored practice on the border frontier; poached native plants the current favorite after drugs. The penalties made it a risky practice—not that Sam would shy away from a little risk; he seemed to thrive on it.

"Is your permit still valid?"

"Not only valid, but extended," he said with a smirk. "I'm collecting native plants from several ranchers now who want to clear their land of hazards to cattle, and more to come. You can expand your inventory."

She thought that over and couldn't come up with one rancher who would discuss this with Sam Bassinger. Her eyes slashed toward his. "Cut the bullshit. If you're not running a legal operation I could go to prison right along with you. That's what happened to Sid Ferris over in Pecos. Remember?"

She pushed her chair back a few inches. "My kids need their mother."

"Hey," he coaxed with a low voice. He stood and moved around the desk to where she sat, placing a hand on her shoulder. "Calm down. My dad's a judge. Remember? Think I want to bring shame on his name?"

"Who knows?" she sneered up at him.

They glared at one another.

"All right." Her shoulders sagged in remembering how she needed the money the plants would bring. "What plants do you have?"

He returned to his seat and looked her in the eye. He raised a thumb. "Well, I've got cactus of all kinds: Sotol," he raised one finger at the mention of each plant. "Thompson yucca, Blue agaves, and Spanish daggers."

"Great!" she exclaimed. "All good sellers." She smiled at her good fortune. "When can you deliver?"

Sam looked up slyly from the hat in his hands and drawled, "Well, now ..."

It took her a moment to catch the innuendo. "Come on, Sam, this is strictly business!"

"Yes, ma'am," he countered. "How about tomorrow?"

Susanna's voice and eyebrows lifted. "That quick?"

"Sure. I'm no slouch." He grinned. "How about noon?"

Susanna jumped to her feet. "Same prices as the last delivery?" She did a quick tally in her head. "Per plant?"

"Yep," Sam nodded.

She extended her hand across the desk like a rancher conducting business. "It's a deal. Just make sure you have the proper papers ready with that shipment."

Sam stood and clasped her hand, gently nudging her palm with his thumb. Susanna stood rigid at the sensual feeling.

"You bet," he said. "But I'd rather seal this in another way." He drew her hand to his lips, eyes teasing.

She laughed in spite of herself and then jerked her hand free, angry for letting her guard down. "Get out of here!"

Sam put his hat on and strolled out the door. "Adios." He gave a jaunty, two-finger wave.

"Tomorrow," she shot back, hoping he wouldn't deliver the plants himself.

* * *

Doris sat in the cafe sipping another cup of coffee. She made a decision, collected her walking stick, paid for her lunch at the register, and left. In her little yellow Volkswagen, she drove the short distance to the west side of Alpine where she saw numerous vehicles parked around Frank and Trudy Johnson's frame house: official Highway Patrol cars, a Compton Produce delivery truck, and a Subaru station wagon.

A crisply uniformed patrolman with a clean-shaven face stood by the front door. He lurched to attention, touching his hand to his hat brim in a kind of salute as Doris approached.

"Good afternoon, ma'am."

He turned and rapped the door lightly. A slender, impeccably coiffed woman wearing a beige sweater and matching slacks opened it.

"Come in, Doris," said the preacher's wife.

"Hello, Glenna," Doris said as she entered. The officer pulled the door shut, remaining on outside watch.

Glenna pointed down the short hallway. "Trudy is in her bedroom."

Another young Texas Highway patrolman stood near Glenna, shuffling his feet, hat in hand.

"Jim is with her," Glenna added and turned to the officer. "Professor Kemp, meet Officer Vargas." The uniformed man responded with a soft, "Ma'am," and then quickly averted his serious eyes.

"New sets of these nice young officers have been coming over every two hours." Glenna gave an appreciative smile. "It's a comfort to have them here. Frank's parents live in Odessa, and Trudy's in El Paso," Glenna continued. "It will be a while before they get here. Barrett Compton is in the kitchen putting away eggs, milk, and all kinds of good stuff, and his wife, Jane, is out in the backyard with little Pete."

Glenna, having more than a casual acquaintance with human tragedy as a minister's wife, was calm in her delivery of information

"If it wouldn't interrupt," Doris said, "I'd like to pay my respects to Trudy."

Glenna assured it was no problem and directed her down the narrow hallway to the first open door on the right.

Doris's low heels and walking stick clicked on the linoleum in the silent hallway. She looked through the first bedroom doorway. Trudy sat in an overstuffed chair near a small bedroom window, her head sagging into her hands. Pastor Jim Post knelt beside her, his hand on her shoulder.

"Trudy, to be absent from the body is to be present with the Lord. Frank was on good terms with his maker," he said softly.

"Well, I'm not on good terms with a God who takes good men, like Frank," Trudy said sullenly, locking her arms across her chest.

Doris stood hesitantly at the doorway. Jim raised his head and made eye contact. "Come in, Doris," he said with a welcoming smile.

Doris went to Trudy, bent down, and put her arms around her.

"Oh, Doris," Trudy mumbled into Doris's cape. "He was too trusting."

"Yes," Doris soothed. "And that made him special, Trudy. I'm sure he was loved by everyone." She paused and asked, "Do you know anyone who didn't? Love him?"

Doris pulled back to see Trudy's response, which was to sob fitfully into her crumpled handkerchief.

Doris shrank back. She gave the pastor a guilty look and said timorously, "I'll see you again soon." She headed back down the hall toward the kitchen.

This won't be easy. But I need to get some facts!

* * *

Barrett Compton grew more agitated in the kitchen as he waited for Jane to return from the backyard. He needed to talk to Sam. Well, maybe not Sam, but *somebody*. Who could he trust? His wife of course, but he was too ashamed to confide in her. The preacher? He was a stranger to Barrett.

"I've had enough of this," he moaned aloud, opening the kitchen door to the backyard. "Jane! Let's go!" he called.

He watched Jane catch Pete's hand and walk the child from a swing set to the kitchen.

Barrett closed the door behind them. He stuffed his arms into his jacket and watched Jane help the boy shed his warm layers.

Footsteps sounded in the hallway, and he envisioned Glenna's polished hair, face, and clothes while he trained his eyes on his wife's brown hair, sallow face, and thin plainness—until she smiled. He loved to see her smile. In fact, he loved her lack of self-consciousness about appearances. All of her energy was for others.

He was surprised to see Professor Kemp enter the kitchen. He knew that she taught at the college, but seeing her here threw him. Had she known Frank and Trudy?

Doris met the rancher's eyes. "Hello. Barrett Compton?"

He nodded.

She held out her hand. "Doris Kemp." Doris hesitated, and then asked boldly, "Do you know if Frank had any enemies?"

Barrett's face twitched, and his mouth clamped shut while his eyes darted to Jane. He jerked his eyes toward the front door with a slight tilt of his head in that direction.

Jane's eyes widened, and she turned to stare at Doris. "Surely this can't be personal? Frank was one of the nicest people I've ever known."

Everyone was silent as Jane buttoned her coat and bent down to plant a kiss on the little boy's chubby cheek.

"I'm so happy about what you told me, Pete, about your daddy. He loved you very much."

Pete's small, round face lit up with a smile, his blue eyes glistening.

Barrett felt his heart constrict with misery.

Doris walked over to Pete and crouched down to the boy's level. "Want to go see Mommy now?"

Pete nodded, and Doris picked him up with a grunt. She held the boy and smiled at Barrett. "It's so good of you to bring food."

He looked down. "We'd better be going," he said and looked up at Jane.

Barrett ushered his wife quickly out the front door, nodding farewell to Glenna. They walked down the driveway to the old, white panel truck that had Compton's Produce crudely painted on the side.

Once again he thought he should repaint the truck so it looked more professional for Jane when she drove it to sell eggs, milk, and vegetables raised on their place. Her little business had helped make ends meet in recent years of poor cattle prices. They seemed to always be working; she in the kitchen, laundry room, and garden; he sunup to sundown—and beyond—tending cattle on the range or making repairs around their two hundred-acre ranch, which was small by West Texas standards. All of their hard work seemed to be getting them nowhere.

"What's wrong, Barrett?" Jane asked in almost a whisper, fidgeting with her seat belt.

"Nothin'."

He hated lying to her. She and the children were his whole world, but he couldn't risk losing her respect. He had to get through this nightmare on his own.

Barrett thought of the dust and starkness on the outskirts of Odessa where he had grown up, and where his father was a hard-drinking, hardworking oilfield driller. Words, affection, and every commodity of life were scarce. His momma was picked green, attacked by her heart at age forty. He decided early that when he had a wife, he'd be good to her, and neither she nor his kids would ever know the want that he and his momma had known. He couldn't imagine being with anyone but Jane. He was devoted to her and their children, but he felt that they deserved better. He didn't want to be the failure that his daddy had been—poor and worthless. But right now he felt like a chip off the old block.

"Where were you last night?" Jane whispered.

He heard the fear in her voice, like she sounded when she knew she was pregnant that last year of high school. That had been an ugly time for unwed mothers. They'd married over a weekend in El Paso.

"You're acting funny, Barrett!" Jane's voice rose with a tremor. "Talk to me! I don't know what to think!"

He saw a tear course down her cheek as he sat hard-faced and silent during the long drive to their place in the mountains above Fort Davis.

His thoughts turned to their kids, good kids aged eight to sixteen. Each could sit a horse well and work with roundup. The three older girls helped with daily housework, milked the cows, fed the chickens, and tended a large vegetable garden. And Jake, his youngest ... Barrett often took his son out on the range and talked about everything he knew about cattle and life. He was Jake's hero.

What would Jake think of him now?

They neared the house. He pictured the children in freshly starched clothes and scrubbed faces, catching the yellow school bus early each morning and returning late in the afternoon. The afternoon bus hadn't come yet. He braked in front of their house.

"You go on in," he said as he motioned to Jane with his head. "I'll be there in a minute."

He twisted his head toward the house, painfully aware that it needed paint and a new roof.

Folks are nothin' if they're poor!

Jane said she didn't mind being poor, as long as she and Barrett were together with their children.

But he minded.

He watched Jane's halting approach to the front door and felt anxious about her sadness and concern over him. He knew that she knew he was keeping something from her.

He slammed on the gas pedal. The tires dug below the wetness of the dirt road and kicked up dust. He drove the panel truck around back near the barn, stopped with a screech, and snatched his cell phone from his jacket pocket. He pounded numbers.

A low, smooth voice answered. "Hey, buddy, I've been trying to reach you all day."

Barrett felt his face flush. "Buddy? How about telling this *buddy* what's going on!"

"Whoa now, slow down. You're gonna have a stroke."

"Listen! We gotta talk!" Barrett said fiercely.

"Okey dokey."

The flippant attitude infuriated Barrett. "Tomorrow! Meet me tomorrow at Loop Road and Marfa highway. Seven in the mornin'!"

He hit END on the phone. *Son of a bitch's got no feelings!*

He stepped out of the panel truck, popping his head up when his favorite horse, Cowboy, whinnied from the corral. He went to where the big Tennessee walker stood with his head craned over the fence. Barrett rubbed Cowboy's forehead and scratched behind his ears; the horse's silky body felt warm to his chilled fingers.

The horse nuzzled Barrett's cheek with a velvety nose, and Barrett's left arm slipped up around the powerful neck. He buried his face into Cowboy's broad shoulder. After a moment, he straightened up, wiping away his tears along with his emotions on the sleeve of his denim jacket.

He gave a firm pat to Cowboy's sleek neck and hustled toward the house to get into his working clothes.

There's got to be a way out.

* * *

Captain Bill Butler glanced at the clock on the wall of his small office. Five o'clock. It had seemed like five o'clock all the gray-long day.

He'd cancelled the stationed patrolmen shortly after his officers reported the arrival of Trudy Johnson's family.

The pain was only beginning there. His head snapped up at a thump at his open door.

"Time to go home, boss," said a patrolman leaning in the doorway. "Gettin' dark."

Butler nodded. They made eye contact. "Some of us are headed to Zeppie's for a drink," the officer added. "Wanna join us?"

Butler smiled wearily. "Not tonight, thanks. You boys go ahead."

The young man acknowledged him and slipped away.

Butler leaned back in his chair. *Home? This is home.* He sat forward and opened the file on his desk labeled "Officer Frank Johnson" and began to read.

CHAPTER TWO

A steady tap-tap-tapping echoed in the dark. Katherine opened her eyes wide, hands clutching the bed sheet tightly.

Sweet relief, she recognized the sound. It wasn't a nightmare or an intruder, just her dog scratching at the back door. She pushed open books and a goose-down comforter aside and swung her legs out of the high bed. Groggily she sat up on its edge, forcing her eyes to focus on a bedside clock: 7:30 AM.

"What day is it?" she mumbled as she stood and stretched her arms upward, yawning. Time had little meaning since she began living alone.

She opened the wooden window blinds near her bed and squinted at the quasi-light of morning. In one continuous movement, she gathered her blond hair to the nape of her neck, picked up a green stretch band from the bedside table to catch her hair up in a ponytail. She slid her feet into soft, leather slippers, pulled a long winter robe from her closet, and headed toward the back door.

"Thursday. It—is—Thursday." She enunciated each word to the little fluff of white hair who turned happily in circles at her feet.

"Today is grocery shopping day, Bananas. A reason to get up." She smiled at the little dog who eagerly watched her every move.

She unlocked and opened the heavy door and held the screen door ajar. Bananas leapt outside, barking at the October sunrise, which surfaced around eight in the mountains.

Katherine closed the screen door and watched as Bananas bounded through tall buffalo grass, flushed a covey of quail, and tumbled head over heels into butterfly bushes near a six-foot adobe wall.

Bananas had her routine, and Katherine had hers: strong coffee, the morning news, and a comfortable chair to cushion her transition from thoughts of her husband and daughter to the reality of life without them.

She headed straight to the kitchen. Grieving as a way of life wasn't normal. A morning routine helped her feel some sense of normalcy.

She searched inside an overhead cabinet for a particular cup. It wasn't there.

Where has Carmen put that cup?

"You have so many pretty cups," her cleaning lady often said, "and you drink from one that belongs in the trash."

She pushed and pulled dishes in every cabinet looking for that cup. It was nowhere to be found.

Carmen didn't know that Katherine's daughter had made the cup for her during a stay in a locked psychiatric ward when Maureen was a teenager, before the voices in her head finally destroyed her. Remembering caused agitation and twisting in Katherine's stomach, much less telling it.

She pulled open a deep drawer that held mixing bowls and measuring cups, and there it was, the purple cup. She set it on the counter, filled an electric pot with water, plugged it into a wall socket, and began her ritual.

"Ummmmm." The full, rich smell of Guatemalan coffee filled her senses. It was her favorite, purchased regularly from Big Bend Coffee Roasters in Marfa. She made the short drive weekly, visiting Marfa art galleries and picking up fresh roasted coffee beans.

Always an observer—like a sparrow on a barbed wire fence—she knew that the trauma of death had narrowed her view. She found temporary escape through art, old movies, books, and music—transporting her to another place, another time, filling the endless hours.

She rambled toward the study with her steaming cup of coffee and a handful of vitamins as Bananas scratched on the back door. Katherine let the little bundle of fur in and felt cold air glide with her through the doorway. She held the door open and stepped out on the porch, gazing at the pink sunrays filtering through the giant limbs of an Arizona cypress tree beyond her back porch. To the distant right, she glimpsed large buildings on the edge of the Sul Ross State University campus where she imagined Doris sitting in her office.

Bananas crept back out on the porch to join her.

Thoughts of the car that had run Katherine off the road came to her abruptly. It had been dark, and the car had surprised her, but it sure looked like the one she had seen going up to the neighbor's house.

Was it the same car?

"I must go up there and get the license number, Bananas. And call Ambrose. I wonder if it's connected to the murder of that patrolman. It was the same morning."

She let the screen door swing shut behind her as her eyes caught a dazzle of sun rising above Hancock Hill. She walked to the end of her porch and stared beyond the corner of her house to the southwest. Morning light reflected pink on the Davis Mountains across Alpine Valley. So beautiful! It was a powerful contrast to the days of gloom and gray after burying her daughter, moving to Alpine, and watching her husband die a year later. This vast golden land with clear blue skies was serene but alive.

She hadn't known this remote region of Texas until Brann brought her out for a visit many years ago. In the newness of love and marriage, they had flown from Houston to his second law office in Odessa, an oil boomtown on the Western plains.

After checking Brann's office schedule, they retrieved his bright blue-checkered cab and drove south. He wanted to show her the McDonald Observatory perched high in the Davis Mountains.

She saw nothing to recommend this trip for the first hour and a half of driving, unless you were fond of pump-dunking oil wells. Then the sculpted Davis Mountains began to rise with sheer audacity from the desert floor.

On a winding mountain pass south of Balmorhea and its spring-fed lake, the gas gauge betrayed the pair, and the car rolled to a stop amid dry summer weeds off the narrow pavement.

"One of us has to go for gas," Brann stated with a broad, easy smile.

He scanned the little-traveled highway and looked back at her. She was wearing a magenta-colored skirt of thin, crinkled cotton, a matching scoop-necked blouse, and sandals that revealed a deep summer tan.

"*You* could stop a car," he teased in that deep, melodious voice that kept courtrooms spellbound. "Fort Davis is about ten miles away. It's perfectly safe for you to stand by the road and hitch a ride out here."

He always said the unexpected, exuding manly confidence.

"Me?" She searched his eyes. He nodded, caressing hers.

"Why am I so easy!" She laughed and got out of the old four-cylinder with her purse strap draped over her shoulder and walked to the edge of the road. She twisted back, meeting his clear, gray eyes once again.

After several minutes of waiting, she spied a lowrider on the horizon: a standard black automobile with surplus chrome slung low on its tires. She timidly raised her right hand, fingers folded down, and stuck out her thumb. She glanced nervously around at Brann and back in time to spot two wide-brimmed, black hats just visible above the dashboard of the passing car. She turned and gasped as she saw it stop and back up to where she stood.

She glanced uneasily at Brann.

"It's all right," he assured. "You'll be perfectly safe."

He could charm the birds out of the trees.

The passenger window opened, and a wrinkled, leathery face peered out, a thin grin revealing open spaces where teeth should have been. The dark barrel of a man behind the steering wheel leaned across the wizened old man and leered into her face.

"Can I help you?"

"Yes, please. We ran out of gas." She motioned nervously with her hand toward Brann and the blue checker. "Can you take me to Fort Davis for gas?"

There was a slight hesitation.

"Yes, of course," the driver said as he nodded, flashing a toothy grin below an enormous black mustache. "Get in."

He turned to the backseat and said something in Spanish.

She halted and looked once again at Brann leaning against the old checker.

"It won't take you long," he called in solid response. "I'll be right here."

He smiled with casual elegance and waved his arm up and then down to pop the tab of a cold Pearl Lite from their cooler.

The old man opened his door and got out slowly, reaching back to pull his seat forward. Katherine crawled into the back, gawking at a small figure wrapped in a yellow-flowered housecoat, black hair twisted around pink foam curlers. The old lady stretched her lined lips across made-to-order teeth and spewed a stream of Spanish, nothing of which Katherine understood.

Why did I agree to this? He's made me a mark while he hangs back in the weeds—in safety!

She squeezed inside, avoiding jugs filled with water on the floorboard, and sat next to the withered woman on the plastic-covered seat.

Pink rollers bent to the floorboard, and a gnarled finger hooked the handle of a jug.

"Agua?"

"No, thank you." Katherine smiled weakly.

She twisted back quickly for a look out the rear window and waved bye-bye to the man she loved.

Didn't he realize that we might never meet again?

After a few miles of silence, she coughed nervously and ventured bravely, "My husband knows this area well. He's a lawyer and has tried many lawsuits in the courthouses of this region. His name is Brannon Bell."

The men in the front seat exchanged a look and chorused, *"Sí!"*

More miles of silence.

"Where do you live?" she tried.

The old man and woman grinned, their heads bobbing in cordial incomprehension.

The large man at the wheel said, "We live in Presidio."

"On the border," she said as she nodded, remembering the map she had recently viewed. Presidio was a small town bridging Mexico at the

Texas river border. Brann had described it as being the poorest county in Texas.

"*Si, senora*," he answered.

Several minutes later they reached the tiny mountain town of Fort Davis and bumped off the road in a cloud of dust at a small grocery store with two gas pumps.

Katherine could still picture that frail old man pumping gasoline into a plastic jug for her. She had followed him inside the store and stood in line at the checkout counter. He quietly held his wrinkled hand up to stop her from paying. He pulled a worn, hand-tooled billfold from his hip pocket and searched hidden recesses to withdraw a small, paper square. Slowly he unfolded it again and again, ceremoniously placing a one-hundred-dollar bill on the counter, smoothing it with both hands. The cashier rang up eighty-nine cents for gas and gave him change.

Without a word, the family took her back to Brann at the pass. She had been so frightened of those sweet, gentle people. She thought of a line by Gilbert and Sullivan: "Things are seldom what they seem." She waved and watched the family from Presidio disappear down the narrow highway.

Now she shivered. She'd been lost in memory long enough to be chilled through and through. "Come on, Bananas. Let's go inside."

Bananas wagged her tail and raced inside as Katherine opened the door. Katherine followed, her sight resting on the living room hearth. *It wouldn't be long—if not now—for a cozy fire. But this was the desert. Where did people find wood?*

Katherine pulled her robe tighter and slipped into the burgundy leather chair near the expanse of windows. Her view spanned the back acre of land and the rise of Hancock Hill. Her thoughts turned again to Brann, the love of her life. Twenty-five years after that first trip to Fort Davis, here in Alpine, she had held Brann's hands in his final moments.

"I'm fine," he said strongly.

"You do know that I love you," she whispered, looking earnestly into those beautiful gray eyes.

He nodded slowly and looked away. Unexpectedly his head fell back and his mouth gaped open. He was gone.

Katherine turned to the sounds of Bananas's diligent pawing and pushing pillows around on the sofa, making a proper nest for a nap. Below Katherine's long windows were shelves crammed with books, more along an entire back wall. Her Stickley side table held a lamp, its shade in stained rectangles of glass a la Frank Lloyd Wright, and stacks of earmarked books and news magazines.

She clicked the TV remote. CNN spouted the morning news. She sipped the rich, hot coffee, sleepily tousled her hair loose from the ponytail band, and heard of more American casualties in wars across the planet, more terrorist cells found in the United States and abroad, more scandals in Washington. Those stories were followed with coverage of a gun rampage in a public high school, a burning chemical plant in North Carolina, a train wreck in Texas, and a blizzard in upper New York State. Her stomach roiled. All the stories were taking place somewhere other than here. Far West Texas didn't exist or was simply not considered newsworthy back East or out West where satellite channels originated.

"They're probably all connected to global warming anyway," Katherine mocked, clicking the television off.

She went to her bedroom, thinking again about the shock and local buzz of the murdered patrolman. There was nothing on TV about it. The local weekly paper had almost no information.

Katherine wondered why Doris wanted to be involved. It was bizarre to her, but she wanted to stay connected to her only friends in town, as well as get connected in the community. Maybe she and Doris could go out to the spot where the young officer was killed and learn something to help in the "investigation," as Doris had called it.

Or better yet, she might first inquire about her neighbors. That could be a beginning. She dialed Doris from her bedside phone and left a message on the recorder: "Hi, Doris, this is Katherine. Just wanted to apologize for walking out on you and

Susanna yesterday. When you have a moment, please give me a call. I really need to talk to you about my neighbors."

She dialed a second number, which was answered on the first ring. "Pioneer Nursery."

"Hi, Susanna. I was hoping that I'd catch you."

"Katherine! Are you OK?"

Katherine felt embarrassed about her behavior and how emotional she had become. "I'm fine, and I apologize for leaving yesterday. I can only hope it didn't spoil your lunch with Doris."

"Oh, no. I understand. I'm glad you called. It gives me a break from bookkeeping. But tell me, what's the big deal? I understand you have a *mystery* you've been keeping to yourself."

Katherine could picture Susanna leaning back in the chair at her office desk with her boots kicked up.

"Well ..." Katherine stalled. "Let's all get together and talk about it. I think it's serious. How about tomorrow? Can you leave work a little early?"

"Let me check my calendar."

Katherine heard Susanna's boots scrape near the phone and her chair screech with movement.

"Here it is. Sam's delivering plants today. Leroy and I could have them displayed by tomorrow noon."

"Do you worry about the cold fronts coming in?" Katherine asked.

"Well, Leroy and I need to get a covering over the herbs and fragile plants before more cold weather sets in, but yes. I could get away by mid-afternoon tomorrow."

"About three?"

"Sure. Clay's practice is after school today."

"Good! Let's meet on my back porch, if the weather's pretty. If not, we'll meet inside. I'll let Doris know. See you soon."

As Katherine put the phone down, it rang.

"Hello." She changed the phone to her left ear and gathered a pencil and pad. It was Judge Bassinger telling her he lived nearby, and that his son, Sam, was her next-door neighbor. Then he proceeded to talk about her need for a new trash bin and locating it next to her house.

What a weird call. Why on earth would this man, a judge, care about my Dumpster? Was there another reason for his call? Really. Would I like my trash bin closer to my back driveway?

She walked into her second bedroom, now made into an office. Bananas followed and laid down on the long pillow on the floor near Katherine's computer.

Katherine glanced at the closet door.

I need to sort through those boxes of Maureen's things. But I don't think I can. Not yet.

She sat at her computer and e-mailed Doris about the meeting time tomorrow. Then she decided to call to her brother, Ambrose.

"Surely he'll know how to get that license number," she said to Bananas as she dialed. "Or maybe we'll just sneak up there and look for ourselves."

* * *

"Whoopee! I made it! I made it!"

Susanna's gangly ten-year-old son hurtled toward her. He flung his arms around her, crushing the grocery bag she held. When Clay pulled back, Susanna's heart squeezed as she saw her husband's face, dark wavy hair, his amazing eyelashes, and enormous dark eyes.

"Made what?" Clay's older sister asked, looking up from her homework spread across the dining room table.

Susanna realized once again how much her lovely teenage daughter reminded her of her own mother—all but that black hair—with a fair Scottish complexion and green eyes, *and* a confrontational attitude.

"The team! The team!" Clay jumped with excitement tossing an imaginary ball into a fantasy hoop.

"What team?" Lisa asked.

"The basketball team, dummy!" He scowled.

He turned quickly to Susanna. "And I have to get to practice soon, Mom!"

Susanna pushed the door shut behind her with a shove of her boot heel, balancing grocery bags, coat, keys, and a purse in both arms.

"Do you mean that little squirts like you play *basketball*?" Lisa looked amazed.

"I'm not a squirt!" Clay stood his ground. "Mom!" he pleaded.

"Hey, hey, you guys! Cut it out. Give me a hand with these bags, please."

Lisa shrugged and backed her chair away from the table in the area that was both living and dining room. She rushed to her mother in time to catch a slipping grocery bag.

Susanna moved into the kitchen to set the bags on the counter. "Thanks, darlin'. How was school today?"

"OK," Lisa chirped.

Susanna accepted that teenagers gave no real information unless interrogated.

"Can we eat out tonight? Please?" pleaded Clay. "I *hafta* get to basketball practice on time!"

"You know we can't afford to do that. We'll make it. Hurry and set the table," she said as she motioned to him.

Great kids, she thought as they pitched in to help her unpack grocery bags at the kitchen counter.

We were a great team: Marcos, me, and the kids.

She thought of Frank Johnson's widow. Her world too had turned upside down.

She placed a package of plastic-wrapped ground beef and a carton of eggs next to the big gas range. She treasured that stove of stainless steel with six burners, a griddle, and two ovens. It was the first really nice appliance that she and Marcos had bought for the old house they'd remodeled together after Clay was born. And the house was almost paid off. She searched for a large frying pan in the lower cabinet.

Her hand grasped the handle of a skillet, and she stopped for a moment, realizing that this was the time of day that Marcos would have been getting home to join the family for dinner. To her surprise, the sharp pain that usually accompanied these thoughts was missing.

She opened the carton of eggs, remembering how she had told Doris only last year, "My heart is shattered. Like glass. Piercing every breath, every memory."

Doris had nodded. "I understand."

Would Doris understand this easing of pain? Sure she would. But then again, Doris had recently confided that she had actually been relieved when her husband died.

The egg she held to mix with hamburger meat slipped to the floor, splattering yellow yolk and glossy egg white across the Saltillo tile floor.

Wish I had a maid like Katherine has!

"Mommmm!" Clay whined loudly. "We have to hurry, or I won't be on time!"

"OK, OK. Help me clean this up. We'll make it."

CHAPTER THREE

The morning was cold with fog dipping low in the Davis Mountains. Little traffic was out but for ranchers taking bags of feed out to the range for hungry cattle.

Barrett drove his old, rusty pickup from the ranch house above Fort Davis and slipped into memories of himself as a kid going out on his grandfather's barren range in winter to feed the cows. Gramps would drive the pickup loaded with bags of feed through the gate of a certain pasture and honk, honk, honk. The cows would come running! In a bad winter, those critters would not only eat the scattered feed, which looked like cubes of dry dog food, but they'd eat the paper sacks too.

He popped the steering wheel with his fist. "God, what a tough life!"

He spied Sam's new truck at the crossroads and swerved onto the easement next to him and cut his engine.

Sam's window glided open. "Get in," he called to Barrett and flicked a cigarette butt to the ground.

Barrett got out of his truck, dust flying around his worn work boots.

Sam saw a flash of faded jeans and a flannel shirt as his partner crossed behind his truck in long, swift strides.

Barrett jerked the passenger door open and faced Sam with clenched teeth. "I didn't get into this deal for no killin'! What the hell's goin' on?"

Rasputin bristled and growled from the pickup bed, moving toward Barrett.

"Remember it right, Barrett!" Sam pointed a finger in Barrett's face. "You and me loaded those plants we dug up from the park into that semi, and we *left*!"

Barrett's callused hands clenched into fists. "Well, count me out! Collectin' ordinary desert plants where there are lots of 'em is one thing. This is somethin' else!"

Sam thrust out his bottom lip up and crossed his arms, staring out the windshield.

"I need the extra money. Bad!" Barrett raged. "But I don't want no part of this!"

Sam faced him again and said slowly, "You're already part of it, pal. We just gotta wait this out."

Barrett glared back at him.

"Keep your head." Sam tried to smile. "Be smart. Stay cool."

"Fine words, Sam," Barrett sneered. "You and your big ideas. Well, this ain't what I thought. Don't you think you can't go to prison even if your old man *is* a judge!"

He backed away from the door and slammed it fiercely, yelling, "Don't call me, Sam! Don't ever call me ag'in on any of your deals!"

Rasputin barked and jumped up, placing his big puppy paws on the tailgate. He hung halfway out of the truck to yap furiously at Barrett, who tracked defiantly back to his own vehicle.

Sam slammed the steering wheel with his open palm, dug a cigarette out of his shirt pocket, and leaned forward to light it in his cupped hands. He lifted his Stetson and shoved his falling dark hair from his face. He drew deeply on the cigarette.

Barrett was back in his old truck and heard Sam burn rubber out to the highway. He looked up just in time to see Rasputin nearly fall out of the back. He kept staring until the big pup regained his footing and moved up behind the cab, his tongue waving in the wind.

* * *

Sam sped toward Marfa, pushing numbers on his cell phone.

"Armando!" he roared. "I need you to grab your cousin and make a delivery.

"Today at noon.

"The plants in my barn.

"Damn it to hell!" he shouted. "*All* of 'em!"

He pulled more smoke down his throat. "Yep. Take 'em on the flatbed to Pioneer Plants in Alpine."

Smoke filtered out through his nose. He spit a piece of tobacco from his tongue.

"I'll put the papers and invoice in the cab pocket ready for you to give Ms. Perez. Got that?"

He snapped the phone off and tried to relax, checking himself in the rearview mirror and then glancing at Rasputin who was watching him through the cab window.

"Get rid of the evidence, they always say. Miss Susanna will be pleased."

* * *

"Pull the truck into the back driveway," Susanna yelled as she pointed toward the south side of the nursery.

The thin Latino youth nodded and drove around to the side entrance of Pioneer Nursery. Susanna stood on the curb with her arms folded across her chest, watching. A second Latino jumped from the back of a flatbed truck fitted with high sideboards. He opened the nursery's ten-foot-tall gates, pushing them open wide enough for the truck to back through. The driver entered and parked, and Susanna followed the truck. She saw the driver reach into the dashboard pocket and clutch a set of papers in one hand. Then he got out of the truck and looked around for her.

She unfolded the papers the young man handed to her and reviewed them to check the invoice against the plants as they were unloaded.

These look too good to be true. And so many! Now how did Sam get this many native plants?

She glanced down at the invoice attached to the permission sheets. *The papers looked authentic enough.*

* * *

Katherine stood on the back porch and waved as Susanna approached the wrought iron gate to her backyard. Bananas raced over with her tail waving.

Susanna was closing the gate behind her when Doris arrived, and together they ambled toward Katherine's back porch that faced Hancock Hill.

"Keep your jackets on, girls," Katherine advised. "It's a bit chilly. Maybe too chilly?"

"No, no," they responded.

Katherine guided them to a round teak table on the open porch. She raised her eyes at the canopy above the mountain behind her. The bluebird sky was cloudless. Clear light crisply defined the vegetation and geologic matter with singular expression. Expanses of Golden three-awn and Feather grass, volcanic rocks and fissures, Sotol spikes and Prickly Pear cactus posed in shafts of burnished sunlight like a painting. "It's easy to see why people come to Far West Texas," she said with a sigh.

"You have an oasis of grass and flowers, Katherine. Your climbing roses are still blooming in October? Are they Don Jeans?"

Katherine smiled. "No, they're called Blaze."

"And trees!" Doris exclaimed. "What are those big, gorgeous ones by your back driveway? On the south side, with leaves of red, gold, and yellow?"

"Those are Pistachio trees. Their leaves are turning and will soon drop for winter."

Katherine was pleased that her friends enjoyed the yard. It brought so much peace and beauty to her tangled maze of feelings.

"And your field of lavender is *stunning*!" Susanna added, pointing to a patch at the lower end of the yard. "What a healthy stand." She drew a deep breath. "The fragrance is intoxicating, even this late in the year!"

Doris stood and clasped her hands like a child, marveling at a multitude of fluttering yellow wings among the tall points of lavender. "Look! It's blooming butterflies!"

"The monarchs have been coming through, stopping off for a nip from those butterfly bushes." Katherine pointed out the greenery that Bananas had tumbled into yesterday. "It will all be gone soon."

She remembered her hostess duties. "Tea or coffee?"

"An herbal tea sounds good," Doris said with a smile.

"Strong coffee—with cream, if you have it," Susanna said.

"Got it." Katherine nodded and went through the door that led into her big, modern kitchen.

She poured boiling water over a tea bag to steep in a china cup. She chose a matching cup for Susanna's coffee.

Brann and I were in London at that famous department store when I bought these tall cups with hand-painted red and black berries.

For a moment she lapsed into memories.

"Ask her what the *mystery* is," Susanna whispered to Doris as they sat together on the porch.

"Give her time. She'll tell us."

Katherine returned to the porch with a tray laden with steaming cups, sweeteners, thick cream, and scones from the Sixth Street Bakery. There were also spoons, napkins, and a vase of flowers. She was happy that she could make things beautiful. She set the tray deftly on the table, picking up the slender vase of fresh-cut lavender to place in the center.

"Brann used to say, 'All we have left in the end are memories.' So let's make good ones today." She joined her friends at the table.

"This is about the age when memories catch up with you," Doris quipped. "If they're not good ones, they'll kill you."

The ladies laughed knowingly and prepared their drinks.

After a few minutes, Katherine leaned over the table and said in an exaggerated whisper, "It's my *neighbors*!"

Doris and Susanna leaned toward her.

"You both know there are no streetlights within a half mile of this house, and the nights are pitch dark but for stars," Katherine began.

"Dark enough for one of the largest telescopes in the northern hemisphere to be housed at McDonald Observatory in the Davis Mountains," Doris reminded them.

"Oh! That's what Marcos and I loved most to do with the kids," Susanne mused wistfully. "Take them up to the observatory on Stargazer Nights and sit in that circle on the mountaintop while our guide named and pointed to every star and galaxy with a red laser beam."

"Yes. I love that too," Doris agreed. Both women's eyes glazed over with memories.

"Well," Katherine spoke through the enchantment. "I rarely see my neighbors. But the change of behavior by one neighbor to the north has piqued my curiosity." She aimed her index finger toward a large red-tile roof sitting high and solitary on the mountainside.

They all stared at the house on the hill.

"The Burkson house," Doris acknowledged.

"Yes," Katherine agreed. "Well, it's been lighted all around the outside at night, every night, for two years. *But* since early September, it's been in darkness. Every night."

"And it's now October!" Susanna's eyebrows rose as she stated the obvious.

"I've never met the people who live there, but I'm told that an elderly man and his wife share the house."

"That's right," Doris confirmed. "The Burksons built that house over a three-year period, and then moved to the area about fifteen years ago when Mr. Burkson retired as CEO of an oil company in Houston. A friend at the university told me about them, and I think I told you, Katherine."

"Yes," Katherine said. "Promptly at eight o'clock each morning, every morning, for the past year, a black automobile came down that drive." She motioned beyond the adobe wall to the back cedar fence of her acre.

"The car has tinted windows, so I don't know who's driving. Then for two weeks, it didn't appear at all, and now I rarely see it. But recently I saw a sports car go up there, and I haven't seen it go out."

Susanna set her coffee cup down abruptly. "How old are the Burksons? Maybe someone's ill?"

"Well, I was worried too. When that sports car arrived, I decided to hike up the hill to visit, or at least try to get the license plate number of that car. I can't be sure, but I think I've seen it before … trying to run me off the road!

"My brother suggested that I wait on him to go up and look around, but he's so busy with that murder investigation."

"Did you see them? The Burksons?" Doris put down the scone she held and looked eagerly at Katherine.

"That house is almost impossible to approach because of high walls," Katherine said.

Again they looked at the house on the hillside.

"The driveway gate was open, so I went through. I passed a triple-car garage, and one door was open for me to see their black car. I peeked inside. It was the only car there. So I went around to the small concrete porch and rang the doorbell."

Katherine stopped and took a sip of hot tea.

"And?" Susanna prodded.

"No one answered," Katherine said and set her cup down. She told them how she had looked through the long, narrow windows on either side of the door and had seen wide marble floors and lights on inside the house. She had heard the bell ring inside when she rang a second time, but she didn't hear or see anybody.

"So, did you call the police?" Susanna asked.

"I did. They checked, and then called back to say that they had spoken with Mr. Burkson and that all was well."

"Why don't *we* check around?" Doris suggested. "It might not have been Mr. Burkson who answered. Did the police go by the house, or did they just call?"

"They didn't say, but I think somebody just called the residence and spoke to whoever answered because I never saw a police car go up there."

"It could be the people are just getting old and not going out much," Susanna said.

Doris nodded agreement.

"I don't know," Katherine said. "But I'm determined to find out."

It was quiet but for the clink of cups as the women finished their drinks.

"Tomorrow morning is Frank Johnson's funeral," Doris said.

"Are you really getting involved with that murder investigation?" Katherine queried.

"Well, it *is* an opportunity to put into practice what I've read about crime investigations and taught all these years," Doris said. "In fact, does anyone want to go with me now to view the murder scene?"

"Now?" Susanna squeaked.

"I will," Katherine answered, determined to be included, even though she felt a little disappointed at the abrupt change of subject from her neighbors. "I've been thinking the same thing—about going out there with you." She stood and collected the cups onto the tray she had carried out earlier. "Just give me time to put these dishes away."

Susanna began to help, and they whisked everything into Katherine's kitchen, returning quickly to the back porch.

"Sorry," Susanna said as she frowned, "but I can't go. I have to pick up Clay and get dinner ready." She gathered her large leather purse and swung it over her shoulder.

"Are we still on for the art opening in Marfa Saturday night?" Doris asked.

The women nodded and smiled in agreement.

Susanna turned at the gate. "Can we meet and sit together at the funeral in the morning?"

"I'll pick you and Doris up in the morning," Katherine said.

After Susanna left, Doris looked at Katherine. "Shall we take my car now to take a look around?"

"Sure, if Bananas can ride with us."

"Of course," Doris said before getting her purse and walking toward the gate.

"I'll be but a moment getting her leash," Katherine said. She hurried inside.

Bananas turned in gleeful circles on the porch until Katherine returned and hooked the leash to the leather collar decorated with old buffalo nickels.

Doris sat waiting in her small Volkswagen. Katherine and Bananas joined her, Katherine in the front and Bananas on the backseat. Doris headed toward Marathon.

Katherine drank in the beauty of the rolling grassland along the highway. "The light is so *white* out here!"

"You have the eye of an artist, Katherine," Doris said.

"I used to paint," Katherine said wistfully.

"What did you paint?"

"Mostly landscapes. I love the land, especially the mountains."

"Why not now?"

"I can't seem to get interested—or concentrate on *anything*. Maybe I'll paint again one day."

Bananas dozed, sounding gentle snores, as the women rode without speaking.

"Look! Look beside the road!" Katherine exclaimed, pointing to the left side of the highway on the outskirts of Alpine. "Can we pull over?"

Doris signaled a left turn, slowed, and crossed Highway 90 onto a newly cleared parking area below a small, grassy ridge. About twenty yards beyond the fence line was a sweeping formation of hundreds upon hundreds of white tombstones.

Doris stopped the car and looked out the windshield. "What is this?"

She and Katherine cracked their windows and got out, closing the sleeping pup inside. They moved slowly, solemnly, toward a coffin-sized box painted with a draped American flag. Small, white stones, visible only to foot traffic, bore the words, "Big Bend Veterans for Peace."

"I've heard about this," Doris whispered. "The group began with 342 tombstones—that was the number of Texas fatalities in Iraq at the time—with a small army of volunteers helping fabricate the tombstones out of papercrete, a mixture of shredded paper and soupy concrete."

Their eyes scanned the horizon. As far as they could see were replicas of individual sepulchers memorializing each man and woman from Texas who had died in the Iraq war.

"I remember reading in the *Big Bend Sentinel* about the local chapter of Veterans for Peace creating this memorial as their stance against war," Katherine said in a quiet voice. "There are so many."

"Yes. No wonder Scripture tells us to take care of widows and orphans."

"And also those damaged vets returning home," Katherine added.

Quiet moments passed as they stood gazing at the scene before them, and then the two women turned quietly to make their way back to the car where Bananas lay dreaming with little kicks and moans on the backseat.

Doris entered Highway 90 again, driving silently east toward the location the weekly newspaper had reported as Frank Johnson's murder. She watched her mileage gauge for accuracy. About fifteen minutes later, she slowed and pulled off to the right side of the pavement and stopped.

"Is this it?" Katherine asked as she sat forward.

"I think so," Doris said, looking around.

Katherine stepped out of the car and pulled the seat forward for Bananas, who jumped out into the crisp air and fading sunlight. Katherine kept a grip on the leash as the dog trotted along, sniffing the ground. Bananas tugged Katherine forward and began circling, poking her nose into dry gramma grass near the highway. Her actions grew frantic as she focused on a single spot.

"Doris," Katherine called softly over her shoulder. "I think it was here."

Doris, searching the grounds nearby, stopped and looked at Katherine and the dog. She hesitantly approached Bananas, who was standing over a spot with her nose burrowed in the grass.

"Here?"

"I think so," Katherine whispered. She looked beyond Doris toward the Glass Mountains without seeing, wondering if blood could cry out from the ground. She imagined the patrolman as he lay dying in the dark with no one to see, hear, or comfort him.

"I'm so thankful to have been with Brann in his last moments," she said, staring down at the patch of grass where Bananas lay whining. Doris stood by in silence.

Katherine tugged at the leash, and Bananas reluctantly followed her along the highway easement for a ways. She could hear Doris pacing the area and glanced back to see her jotting notes in a small notebook.

Katherine led Bananas back to the vehicle. Once inside, she remembered how a friend had quoted Ecclesiastes after Brann's death: "To everything there is a season, and a time to every purpose under the heaven; a time to be born, and a time to die ..."

Was it Brann's destiny to die that day? Maureen? This young trooper? What about all those white tombstones on the hill? Did personal choice commingle with others' actions to create the fate of every living man, woman, and child? She closed her eyes.

The driver's door creaked, and Doris plopped onto the seat. Before Doris could turn the ignition key, Katherine asked in a low voice, "Do you believe that the spirit lives on? Even after the body dies?"

Doris looked steadily at Katherine. "I believe that the spirit returns to God who gave it."

"And what about those left behind?"

Doris turned in her seat. Her voice was gentle. "Everyone and everything is transitory on this small planet. I believe that life is a gift, and we should live it reverently, joyfully, and thankfully."

CHAPTER FOUR

"Texans sure know how to say good-bye," Susanna said, watching Texas Highway patrolmen line the sidewalk from the entrance of the little, wood-framed church to its parking lot.

Bouquets and sprays of fresh flowers overflowed the church as more than four hundred people filled the small sanctuary and fellowship hall, spilling out onto the church grounds for Frank Johnson's funeral.

The organ quietly played "Just a Closer Walk with Thee."

Katherine sucked in her breath. She remembered telling Brann's law office investigator of many years, "Brann took so much of me with him." And John had responded, "But, oh, he left so much of himself with you!" *Did Brann still walk with her?*

Next to Katherine, Doris sat with a slightly quivering upper lip. If she could only stop comparing these days with the past, let go of *longing* for the same acceptance here as she'd felt in the Texas Valley. She thought of Susanna's recent story about how people caught monkeys in the South Pacific. They'd place a trinket inside a coconut through a small opening, and the monkey would reach in, grab the trinket, and not be able to get free of the coconut while it held the object in its fist. The monkey couldn't climb very well with a coconut on its fist, and was, therefore, easy to catch. Funny how little stories roamed the mind, applying themselves to your own situations. When Doris heard that story, she related the trinket to her time in Edinburgh, Texas, at the University. And then she thought of her husband. His illness was the reason they had had to move. He had been a high school English teacher, long retired when they met. They had had little in common, she now realized, but they had shared the love of travel. They had traveled the world like gypsies, but she had adjusted to him being gone. In fact, she had adjusted very well.

Susanna's mind flashed to a series of childhood scenes with her best friend, Marcos: riding horses; playing kick-the-can; shooting marbles, quail, and coyotes; measuring each other's height on the doorpost as they grew up together on the Passmore spread in the Texas Panhandle, she the rancher's daughter, and he the foreman's son. She had always loved him. During puberty they saw less of one another, restrained by her mother. Her mother's will prevailed until Susanna left home for Texas Tech, where Marcos, a senior and outstanding student in range management, was waiting. Her mother died of breast cancer before their wedding, and Susanna would always wonder if her mother would rather die than see her daughter marry beneath herself.

"Good thing we came early." Katherine's voice, noticeably jagged, broke the reverie.

Susanna stiffened, feeling guilty for her thoughts toward her mother. She nodded at Katherine and tried to concentrate on the here and now instead of the past. She saw that Doris wore an attractive black pantsuit and sported not only a stylish new haircut but also earrings! And her woolen wrap was a solid, deep purple. *Thank God it wasn't the red or yellow cape.* Katherine wore a plain navy dress with heels. Susanna decided that she, too, was appropriately dressed in a tailored brown pantsuit with brown boots.

From a back pew where she and her friends were squished together, Susanna shifted her gaze to the front of the church. She leaned forward to whisper to Doris and Katherine, "Can you see the photographs up front?"

Each craned their neck for a clear look at what Susanna was talking about—a large portrait of Frank in full uniform; his diplomas and awards; and a board filled with photos: Frank as a baby, a high schooler, a groom, and a proud Texas Highway patrolman. The display was placed near the casket.

They could see Trudy and her toddler sitting in a front pew alongside her parents, Frank's parents, and his sisters and grandparents.

Susanna sighed during an overly long eulogy by the preacher. It was followed by emotional tributes from state and local politicians, fellow patrol officers, family, and friends. She was exhausted.

The organ played "A Mighty Fortress Is Our God," and uniformed pallbearers bore the casket behind an officer hoisting a large American flag down the center aisle and out the double front doors.

"I don't think I'll go to the cemetery," Katherine said as the ceremony ended, and they moved with the crowd outside.

"I'm sure the whole town will hear the buglers play 'Taps,'" Doris said matter-of-factly. "Sounds echo through this valley."

The women made their way back to Katherine's SUV in the parking lot, each lost in a personal sea of sadness. They piled into the car, and Katherine backed out of the parking space.

They watched the flashing lights as numerous highway patrol officers, local police, and sheriffs' cars escorted a fleet of automobiles from the service.

"That's a long line going to the cemetery," Susanna noted as she watched Texas Rangers signal passing traffic to pull over. Many drivers got out of their vehicles to stand reverently. "Lisa and Clay said that all the kids would be gathered in front of the elementary school holding flags and flowers as the funeral line passes." She tugged to fasten her seat belt.

"The smaller the town, the bigger the ceremony for heroes," Doris said.

All were silent as Katherine took a back exit from the parking lot.

"Did I tell you about my visit with Frank Johnson's little boy, Pete?" Doris asked.

"No. Tell us," Susanna said, still wrestling with her seat belt.

"I took him to Kokernot Park yesterday so he could run and play awhile," Doris said. "I knew Trudy needed to get ready for this service today." Doris paused as Katherine suddenly pulled the car to the side of the road and stopped, leaving the motor running.

"Go on," Katherine said. "I want to hear this."

"He *wanted* to talk about his dad," Doris continued. She drew her brows together in a look of perplexity. "And he told me something funny."

No one spoke for a moment.

"Like ha-ha funny?" Susanna asked cautiously.

"No," Doris answered ponderously. "Strange funny."

They waited.

"He told me that his daddy came to see him that morning."

"I believe him," Katherine said and gripped the steering wheel.

They quietly waited for Doris to continue.

"Pete said that his daddy stood at his bedside in his officer's uniform," Doris continued. "'He called me Little Bit,' Pete said, and then said to me, 'Daddy said it's because of judgment that he went away.'"

Katherine gasped. The ladies looked at one another, bafflement etched on each face.

"I don't think we can understand some of the things three-year-olds talk about," Susanna said, shaking her head.

* * *

Thick, white clouds rolled down the mountainsides, filling the savannahs with mist, as Katherine made her way to Marfa Saturday evening. She and Doris listened to Marfa Public Radio and the nostalgic sounds of "Always on My Mind," sung by Willie Nelson.

"I miss seeing antelope on this trip," said Doris, searching golden pasturelands on either side of the road.

"Oh, aren't they beautiful!" Katherine said. "I usually see them alongside the highway every time I drive to Marfa, but they're hidden in this fog."

They approached a small tourist watch station with a sign: Marfa Lights.

"Have you seen the lights?" Katherine asked.

"Yes. Once." Doris stretched her neck forward to look out Katherine's window as they passed the tiny building on the south side of the highway. "It's not a tourist trap," she said. "Those round, bobbing lights have been seen and sightings recorded for more than a hundred years."

"What do they look like?" Katherine asked.

"I saw them one night looking to the southeast from that viewing porch." Doris turned sideways and pointed back toward the small, brick building. "They were white circles of light that bounced up and down, fairly near the earth, in sets of two to five across. Then they would disappear and reappear in different places. Very strange."

"What do you think they are?" Katherine snapped her eyes back to the highway as she continued west to Marfa.

"There are many theories. NASA scientists, Japanese scientists, all kinds of people, have come to observe the phenomena over time. None has an explanation. I think it's a magnetic field. There are other magnetic fields known on the planet."

"Another mystery," Katherine said with a sigh. "I feel cloaked in mystery."

The spire of the historic Presidio County Courthouse on the Marfa town square emerged through the clouds as they slowed on the outer fringes of the town. They coasted into Marfa past adobe houses and decades-old businesses and saw a crowd gathered outside of Skywatchers, a gallery located on the left side of the highway going west through town.

Katherine recognized Sam Bassinger leaning against the gallery wall near the front entrance, one boot heel propped behind him. A cigarette dangled from his lips as he faced a young woman with short, red, spiked hair wearing skin-tight jeans cut low to reveal a dragon tattoo rising from below the waist up her backside.

"The usual suspects," Doris said, nodding toward Sam and the group standing around the contemporary gallery.

Katherine glanced toward Doris. "Is Sam related to Judge Bassinger?"

"The judge is his father," Doris answered as she ogled Sam and the young woman. She turned back to Katherine. "Why?"

"I must say, the father has an inordinate affection for Dumpsters."

Doris wrinkled her brow. "What does that mean?"

"Oh, he's been calling me about getting a Dumpster." Katherine turned south and parked the car alongside the gallery.

Doris looked bewildered, but Katherine changed the subject. "Why is this dusty little West Texas town such a big deal in the arts?" She pulled the key from the ignition and opened her door to get out.

Doris shrugged and exited her door. Together they walked toward the entrance.

"Marfa in recent years has attracted nationwide attention for the minimalist art of deceased artist Donald Judd. The stories written in the *New York Times* and various Texas newspapers have brought an influx of wealthy patrons. They buy second or third homes in this little town with its broad, empty streets, not to mention the *ideal* weather," Doris explained.

"It's so weird to see New York–style galleries along Highland Avenue and the intersecting highway," Katherine said, rummaging in her purse for tickets.

Doris nodded. "The largely Hispanic community—before transition—has dwindled to fewer and fewer families. They find the rising sale prices for their adobe homes irresistible. Now only a few remain, and in their place we have restaurants and galleries or getaway quarters."

Katherine showed their tickets at the front entrance and turned to Doris with a grin. "I'll go get the wine?"

"Thanks. I'll take a look at the exhibit."

Some minutes later Katherine weaved through the crowd, holding a glass in each hand above her head. She spied Doris standing alone in a corner.

"Did you see the exhibit?" Katherine asked, handing her a frosty glass of chilled white wine.

"Yes," Doris said slowly and took a sip. "The pieces are so … like art after school. Do you know what they're supposed to represent? Or the statement?"

"I don't have a clue." Katherine laughed softly. "But I do know they're creative. To make a judgment as to whether or not it's art would be presumptuous on my part."

"I guess so," Doris agreed thoughtfully.

"If we grew up retaining that kind of childlike creativity, we could possibly nurture the world," Katherine said.

"What do you mean?"

"It's been said that those who live creative lives are the true communicators in our communities. Perhaps this exhibit is a way to communicate?" Katherine stopped in front of a display.

"Communicate what?" Doris asked.

Katherine smiled and shrugged her shoulders again.

Rock music groaned and blared in the courtyard as the women strolled through the gallery. Katherine greeted several people whom she had met at former fundraising galas in Houston and Austin when her husband was alive. Many owned getaway homes in Marfa and flew their private planes into the small, local airport.

"Let's go," she said to Doris, placing a hand to her forehead. "I'm getting a headache."

Doris leaned closer to hear what Katherine was saying over the din of talk and music. Just then, Ranger Ambrose Trent made his way through the crowd and stopped near the two ladies.

"Sister Katherine," he boomed.

Katherine looked at him with a broad smile. She glanced at Doris. "You know my brother Ambrose, don't you?"

Doris nodded and extended her hand. "Hello. Doris Kemp. Duty or pleasure?"

Trent smiled. "Both, as a matter of fact."

"Ambrose, I want to talk to you about my neighbors," Katherine began. "Something funny is going on with them."

"Sure," he said. "But keep in mind that things get blown out of proportion out here due to boredom and isolation. I can't go on some wild goose chase when I have an investigation in progress."

"Frank Johnson?" Doris queried.

Before he could answer, Katherine placed her hand to her head. "I'm getting too old for this kind of noise. Let's *go*, Doris." She felt heartsick that her brother would blow her off without hearing what she had to say.

Ranger Trent raised his hand to his Stetson and tipped it. "Good night, ladies. About your questions, Katherine, call me tomorrow." He replaced his hat and was gone.

"He's never taken anything about me seriously," Katherine moaned. "Especially since Brann's death. His lack of confidence makes me doubt myself."

"Feel like you may be losing your mind?"

"Exactly!"

"You're not going crazy—you're grieving."

"But Doris, I'm having trouble with things like names and phone numbers and appointments, much less coping with everyday life. Could it be Alzheimer's?"

"Trust me." Doris gave Katherine a quick hug. "I've been there. It's grief."

Katherine smiled. "Let's go to the restaurant."

The widows made their way to the parked car. Katherine clicked the remote to unlock the car doors, and Doris glided onto the passenger seat. "I hope Susanna was able to get a sitter tonight," she said.

Katherine started the engine and looked into the rearview mirror before pulling out from the curb. "So do I. After all, she's not past the tyranny of hormones. She needs to get out at night and meet some nice man."

"And you think she'll meet one here?" Doris asked, lifting her silvery brows.

"Right," answered Katherine with equal sarcasm, turning west at the corner on her way to the restaurant. "You know, there are a lot of good women out there, but not many good men."

Doris laughed quietly. "All the good ones are taken."

Santucci's had a scattering of people in the small dining area and two sitting at the bar. "We got here at the right time," Katherine said, knowing that the edgy New York–style restaurant would be packed after the exhibit opening.

Doris scanned the room. She spotted Judge Bassinger and his wife, Mary, nearby. The judge nodded his head in a friendly manner at Katherine, while his dolled-up wife lifted her head to stare deadpan at Doris.

Katherine blushed while Doris averted her eyes, smoothing her plain sack dress over her bulky hips. Looking away from the Bassingers, Doris spied Sandy Wisner sitting with another young man at a small table. He met Doris's eyes with a wide smile and a bold wave.

"Who's *that*?" Katherine whispered under her breath, watching Sandy's overture.

Doris was noticeably pink of face. She returned a little wave to the man and cast her eyes downward, responding like a ventriloquist with her lips barely moving. "It's Sandy Wisner, a graduate student of mine who is almost young enough to be my son."

"He sure looks happy to see you," Katherine said.

Doris acted a little giddy. "I'm sure he's not taken with *me*. It may be you, Katherine."

"Don't be silly," Katherine said.

A lean young man in black jeans, a black shirt, and a white apron greeted the women and led them to a table for four near the front windows.

Doris recognized someone seated nearby and said in a conspiratorial tone, "Oh! I went by Town Drug in Alpine and asked Billy, the pharmacist," she nodded her head toward an old man, "if he had seen the Burksons lately."

Katherine's surprised smile was accented with raised eyebrows. "You sure don't waste any time."

Doris wedged into a chair against the wall. "I saw Mrs. Burkson there once, getting prescriptions filled."

Their waiter approached the table. Katherine looked to Doris. "I think we should go ahead and order, don't you? If Susanna goes to the opening and we're not there, surely she'll know that we're here."

After ordering, Katherine turned again to Doris. "Now, tell me what they said at Town Drug!"

"Prescription information is confidential," Doris said. "So I purchased a bottle of Tylenol Sleep and paid for it back by the pharmacy. Billy waited on me, and I casually asked if he had seen the Burksons lately."

They were interrupted by the arrival of their drinks and sat silently while the waiter placed the wine on the table along with a basket of bread and butter. He filled their water glasses and darted away.

Doris leaned closer to Katherine and continued her story. "Billy looked at me kind of funny-like, and said, 'Matter of fact, no.' 'Is that unusual?' I asked him, and again he looked at me quizzically and asked, 'Why do you wanna know?' I shrugged and told him that no one had seen them around for a while. He lowered his head while he rang up the medicine and said, 'I understand they were expecting company,' and he moved away, like that ended the matter."

"Their company must have been in *that car*!" Katherine hissed. She waited for Doris to say more, but Doris took a sip of water and remained silent.

"Is that *it*?"

"That's it," Doris answered while her eyes fastened on the front door. "Look who just walked in."

In a rush of cold air, Susanna breezed through the door, followed by Sam Bassinger.

"Hey girls!" she said loudly with a big wave as she spotted Katherine and Doris seated off to the right. "Close the door, Sam."

"Uh-oh." Doris rolled her eyes toward Katherine.

Katherine signaled hello with a smile, lowered her head, and whispered, "What's she doing with *him*?"

Doris smoothed the napkin in her lap and spoke out of the side of her mouth. "We can only hope that he just followed her over here."

The young bartender who worked with Susanna as a substitute schoolteacher waved her over. "Susanna Perez, meet a new resident of the area, Captain Bill Butler and his daughter."

Look out! Susanna thought as she encountered the handsome, middle-aged man. He and the young woman were seated at the bar. *I heard there was a new Texas Highway Patrol captain in town.*

Butler politely stood while they were introduced. Sam, standing behind Susanna, took off his hat and pushed his arm in front of her to shake hands. "Sam Bassinger."

Susanna was embarrassed. "Sam's never met a man who wasn't competition," she murmured under her breath.

"This is my daughter, Clarissa," Butler said, and his chiseled good looks lit up with a smile. "She's a junior in college and visiting for the weekend."

Susanna studied Clarissa. She looked a lot like her dad—tall and thin with almond-shaped, brown eyes. Her brown hair was cut short in a pixie style, and she wore a skin-fitting pullover top that didn't quite reach the jeans that sat low on her hourglass hips.

"Where do you go to school?" Susanna asked with a friendly smile.

"Texas Tech in Lubbock," Clarissa said shyly.

"Ah yes, Lubbock. I spent three days and as many nights there—*one* Saturday," Susanna said dryly and drew a laugh all around.

"Just teasing." She grinned at Clarissa. "Tech is my alma mater."

Sam fixed his eyes intensely on Bill. "Where's the missus tonight?"

Susanna watched Bill and his daughter glance briefly at each other.

"She stopped putting up with me about ten years ago," he stated with a shrug.

"She lives in Galveston," Clarissa supplied. "So I get to visit the coast and the mountains. I never knew there were mountains in Texas before now." She giggled, and Susanna warmed to her.

"I'm joining my friends for dinner," Susanna said, turning and waving again to Katherine and Doris. "Everyone is welcome to join us."

"I think I'll just join the folks here at the bar if they don't mind." Sam took an empty stool next to Clarissa.

"We were just leaving," Captain Butler said. "I needed a real drink after that art opening." Susanna saw him wink at Clarissa.

"It was really hot!" Clarissa was exuberant.

"It was," Susanna agreed. "Well, Sam, see you." She gave a nod his way and looked back at Clarissa and Butler.

"Nice to meet you, Clarissa, and welcome to the region, Captain Butler. I'm so sorry about the death of that young patrolman. There are other things going on in Alpine that I'd sure like to talk to you about sometime." She stepped back.

"Yes, ma'am, anytime," Butler said, looking directly into Susanna's eyes.

She held his gaze and felt herself sway. She pulled her eyes away to glance at Sam who'd turned to the bar mumbling into his glass, "This is not a happy ending."

Susanna joined her friends, and by the time the evening was over, she and Katherine had hatched a plan to talk to Captain Butler, tomorrow if possible, about Katherine's neighbors.

"Sorry. Better count me out this time," Doris said. "I have other plans."

CHAPTER FIVE

The next morning Katherine stood before the expanse of windows in her TV room as the sun rose above Hancock Hill. She noticed the leaves on the young cottonwood trees between her adobe wall and the coyote fence had turned yellow and gold. Her gaze lowered to the ground. She couldn't believe her eyes. There were mule deer in her *yard*—a doe and her fawn. No, a doe and *two* fawns were grazing on buffalo grass.

"Oh, no," Katherine breathed. *Is there a hole in the fence?*

The hand-constructed outer fence of uneven cedar poles wired closely together was supposed to keep deer and other wildlife out.

She opened the coat closet near the back door and pulled out low-cut boots and a light jacket, closed Bananas inside the house, and headed to the back side of her acre.

There she saw not three, but five deer; there was yet another doe with a fawn. All were gray with concise beige, tan, and brown markings on their hindquarters. Both doe, their large eyes luminous and huge ears erect, stood perfectly still and watched warily as she approached.

"Hello?" she said softly. "You shouldn't be in here, you know."

A sudden thunder of hooves outside the fenced area blasted the quietness. A covey of quail shot up like cannonballs with rushing wings. She turned in time to see a small buck, his rack of horns aloft, racing for the field behind her next-door neighbor's house.

"Trying to warn your family?" she called after him.

She grew ever more curious as to how the deer had entered the yard as her eyes followed the lower west fence line. The wrought iron gate was open.

She spoke to the deer. "Uh-oh, Javier must have left the gate open yesterday. You guys had best find your way out quickly. It's not safe around here for you to become tame."

The doe stood like statues, wide eyes watching her while their fawns continued to graze. A neighbor's white cat streaked across the ground, and one tiny fawn pranced after it.

It's like ballet, Katherine thought.

She watched the cat skim under the back fence poles, and as she looked up, the neighbor's sedan drove slowly up the hill. The windows were open, and she could see four faces fastened on the deer: a young man, two women, and a middle-aged man.

Katherine froze like the deer and watched the strangers, trying to memorize their faces so she could describe them to Captain Butler. *Who were these people? Certainly not old enough to be the retired people she had been told lived there. So why are they driving my neighbor's car?*

* * *

Susanna awoke pondering whether she should call Captain Butler. He would be a good resource for information on the Burksons; yet her personal attraction to him made her doubt the logic.

Her phone rang.

Maybe he's calling me!

"Hello," she answered with a catch in her voice.

"Susanna! I just saw that car again! Going up to the neighbor's house! And it was filled with suspicious-looking people!" Katherine was out of breath and talking in gasps.

"So I should call Captain Butler now?"

"Yes! Bring him over this morning if you can."

Susanna hung up smiling. After a shower, she dressed in a new pair of straight-legged jeans, a cream-colored cotton turtleneck pullover, and black Western boots. Her long mahogany hair needed more attention than she had time for, so she pulled it back and clasped it with a large, turquoise-studded barrette. She moisturized her lightly freckled cheeks and applied a natural lip-gloss.

Coffee time.

She clicked the kitchen radio to Marfa Public Radio for *The Morning Edition*. The clock read 9:00 AM as she finished a cup of strong coffee. Time to call the captain.

In spite of feeling foolish, since this was probably a sham for getting to know *him*, she wrote the telephone number from directory assistance on a pad of paper. She sat on the edge of her bed and pressed the numbers in sequence on her phone.

"Butler here," answered an alert, official voice.

"Captain Butler, this is Susanna Perez. Sorry to call this early."

"You can call me at any hour."

Susanna imagined a smile on his craggy, weathered face.

"Well, thank you, Captain."

"Please, call me Bill."

"OK—Bill."

She held the phone and fell straight back on her bed, her stomach quivering. "As I mentioned to you last evening, my friends and I are concerned about some strange behavior in town. It could be connected—it's a long shot—but it could be connected to the murder of Frank Johnson."

She paused.

He remained silent.

"I was wondering if I could talk to you about it over coffee." She sat up on the side of her bed, every muscle in her body tense as she waited for his response.

"I'll be glad to help, but anything within the town limits is handled by the city police department."

I totally misread the signals. But this is for Katherine. "We would be more comfortable talking to you about this first." She hated the coyness in her voice. *Comfortable? Especially since I just met you? Lord, I'm acting like a schoolgirl!*

"OK. It's my day off. When and where?"

"Today?" she asked hesitantly, suddenly unsure of what to think or say.

"Sure. What time?"

"How about ten o'clock this morning at Katherine Bell's house?" She realized that her voice had risen an octave.

"And where is that?"

"She lives on the Loop, near the Sul Ross campus. And Bill?"

"Yes?"

"Thank you." She felt tingly and excited as she returned the telephone receiver to its cradle. She shot both arms above her head. "Yes!"

She hurriedly scrawled a note to the kids:

Hey, sleepyheads, I've gone to Katherine's for coffee. Be back before noon, and we'll go to Pops' Burgers for lunch. Love, Mom

She placed the note under a Carlsbad Cavern magnet on the refrigerator, knowing that Clay went directly there for chocolate milk and Lisa for a Diet Dr Pepper when they awoke.

She dialed Katherine, who picked up on the first ring. "Hello? Susanna?"

"Yes! It's on! Ten o'clock this morning."

"Anyone with you?" Katherine asked.

"Captain Butler is coming." A smile was in Susanna's voice.

"Aren't you something!" Katherine said. "See you soon."

* * *

Katherine placed yellow cotton, woven mats on the glass-top table in the breakfast area of her kitchen. The table was near large windows with a view across her back acre and beyond. She put bright blue, cloth napkins next to the mats and stood a moment looking up the hill. The weather was chilly and overcast with dark, threatening clouds overshadowing that tile roof on the mountainside.

Bananas hovered around her feet, waiting for a treat. Katherine looked from the hillside to him. "What's going on up there? Maybe the Burksons are being starved—or tortured? Old and frail, as Doris indicated, means they couldn't survive long."

She went to the refrigerator and took a small cube of cheese from a Ziploc bag and gave it to her little pal; then she removed pastries from a paper sack and placed them in the oven to warm. The aroma of freshly ground coffee beans filled the kitchen.

She returned to her bathroom for last minute grooming, whisking dog hairs from her black wool slacks and cashmere sweater. Bananas followed, swishing white hair into the air with each wag of her tail.

Katherine picked up the ringing phone in her bedroom.

"Hello, this is Katherine Bell."

"Good morning," said a deep, smooth baritone. "This is Harlan Bassinger."

"Yes. My neighbor," she countered.

What in the world could he be calling about on a Sunday morning?

She carried the phone with her into the bathroom and stood in front of the mirror, whisking a brush through her shiny blond hair.

"Actually, my son Sam is your next-door neighbor. But everyone's a neighbor in Alpine. I thought you might be happy to hear that we have a new waste company in town ..."

"A new garbage company is coming to Alpine?" she asked. *Whoopee.*

She held the phone to her left ear and tried to squeeze toothpaste one-handed and brush her teeth while listening.

"They'll be planning new trash bin sites," he continued. "And you could ask for one near your back driveway."

"Yes, yes, it would be *perfect* to get a Dumpster placed near my house." Her words were fake and mushy with toothpaste. *I don't believe this is happening.*

"I've asked the company to send the surveyors to your house Monday morning," he added.

He sounded so serious. "Yes, I'll remember to look for them," she said, and listened for laughter but heard none.

"Two men will be there early," he said.

Was this a test? "Right, I have it. Monday morning. Thank you." She made a funny face in disbelief.

"I wish you a pleasant weekend," he said heartily.

"You, too. Bye." *What's his problem?*

She put her toiletries away and heard a rapping and Susanna's voice at the back door. "Hello? Katherine?"

"Come in," Katherine hollered back and went to welcome her friend. As she closed the door behind Susanna, the front doorbell rang.

"That must be Captain Butler," Susanna whispered.

"Right," Katherine whispered back. "This makes me feel like I'm fifteen years old again."

They crossed the TV and the living rooms to open the front door. Katherine held the door open wide and extended her right hand. "Hello! Thank you for coming."

The tall man removed his gray Stetson and held it to his side while reaching his right hand to gently shake hers. "Bill Butler."

"Katherine Bell. Please, come in."

Butler ducked through the doorway and into her small foyer.

"Coffee is on in the kitchen," she said over her shoulder, moving in that direction.

She nodded as she glided past Susanna, giving her a look that said, *"He's all yours."*

Butler followed and stopped near Susanna, who stood waiting in the living room. Katherine glanced back and noticed a sudden shyness in Susanna. She turned back toward the kitchen and tried to hear their conversation.

"May I take your hat and coat?" Susanna asked in a small, polite voice.

"Thank you." He removed his coat and handed it to Susanna, who draped it over the sofa.

"Is Clarissa sleeping in this morning? Like most sane people?"

"Of course." He smiled and placed his hat near the jacket.

The pair entered the kitchen just as Katherine began pouring coffee into tall mugs at the kitchen table. She smiled at Bill. "Cream and sugar?"

"Just black, please," Butler answered and sat down at the table.

Katherine placed a plate of hot cinnamon rolls on a hot pad in front of him as Susanna pulled out a chair to sit on Bill's right. Katherine sat to his left.

He crooked his head first at Susanna and then at Katherine. "Now, what's this about?"

"My neighbors," Katherine said. "It began with my wondering if a car I saw going up there was the same one that nearly ran me off the road. It was the same night that Frank Johnson, the highway patrolman, was murdered—when I was run off the road—and I got suspicious about there being strangers, and I *saw* them, up at that house."

She paused before gushing, "I think my neighbors are being held captive!"

CHAPTER SIX

Jane didn't know what to do. Barrett and the children were her life, and life was spinning out of control as Barrett became silent and withdrawn.

"What's wrong?" Her voice was tender, her face tense.

She cleared the breakfast dishes, wiped the oilcloth for crumbs, and poured seconds of coffee into two mugs on the kitchen table.

Barrett was silent.

"Is it finances? Have I said or done something wrong?"

"Nothin'," he said and turned away, his face set in stone.

It seemed like the more she tried to please him, the more he pushed away. She knew that he had recently befriended Sam Bassinger, but lately Sam's very name drove Barrett up the wall.

Barrett left before sunup to ride the range. After the children caught the bus for school, Jane cleared the kids' breakfast dishes and the leavings from making sack lunches.

While the washing machine was going, she mopped the kitchen and bathroom floors and remade her and Barrett's bed. The children had dutifully spread their own beds. The house was tidy and clean—even more than usual.

Wednesday was her normal day to go into Alpine, but she prepared to go today to take fresh eggs. She went to the bathroom mirror and gazed at her reflection. Large, hazel eyes above dark circles stared back. She touched her forehead and jaw, smoothing wrinkles etched by the dry West Texas years.

* * *

Barrett could see his own breath, as well as that of the horse and dog, in the morning chill— little, warm clouds that drifted up and away as they rode out in the early morning.

He appreciated Cowboy's unique, four-beat "running walk," making an especially comfortable ride. He reined the horse through piñon trees and Cholla cactus in the north forty acres of the ranch. Scraps, the family's shaggy black-and-white cow dog, ran alongside.

The rain had cleared through the night, and the sun rose into crystal blue skies and glistened on wheat-colored grasses drying into winter. He tugged on the reins, and his horse halted. Barrett's eyes fixed on the purple mountains rising above the horizon, forming the backdrop of his world.

"I'm a coward, Cowboy."

His face was somber as he gave affectionate pats to the horse's neck. Barrett pressed his knees, and the horse let loose, dark mane and tail sailing in the wind as he ran.

Scraps began barking as they approached a deep chasm where cattle occasionally wandered. Barrett reined Cowboy to a walk.

"Whoa, boy." The walker came to a halt.

Barrett dismounted. Gripping the reins in one hand, he slowly edged to the ravine where Scraps barked nosily and ran along the canyon rim, looking below.

Sure enough, there was a cow about halfway down the canyon wall, standing by a small calf caught in some brush. When the cow saw Scraps, her eyes bulged, and she began a frantic series of bellows.

"Stay," Barrett commanded the dog, looking him in the eye.

Scraps shut up and sat down.

Barrett turned and rubbed Cowboy's soft nose with the same command.

He followed a narrow trail of switchbacks down the slope to the tangled calf. Slowly he approached the wide-eyed cow, saliva streaming from her nose and mouth.

"It's all right, mama. It's all right. We'll get your baby loose."

The mama cow scuttled away a few feet, snorting and jerking her head back toward him, bellowing. Barrett was relieved that she didn't run. If she had, it would likely have resulted in a fatal fall into the gorge.

He pulled at thorny branches until he had cleared the way to gather the calf in his arms and pull it free. The mama continued to scream, her frantic sucking breaths almost as loud as her cries. The calf bawled weakly as Barrett placed his left arm under its head and shoulder. Grabbing the two front legs, he slung his right arm under the calf's butt to hoist it up, holding its hind legs. He had learned the hard way that little hooves could be mighty sharp if left loose to kick. He lifted the calf free of the tangles and began climbing, the moaning cow at his heels.

He was sweating and out of breath by the time he reached the top. After he set the calf down, mama came running up to nuzzle and lead her baby away, stopping shortly to let its nose jab into her milk bag, grab a tit, and suckle.

Barrett pulled off his hat and wiped the rolling sweat from his face on a coat sleeve while watching the reunion. He shoved his hat on again and walked over to Scraps.

"Good dog!" He gave solid pats to her head and ruffled her back. "Good dog."

He tossed the bridle reins up around the saddle horn, put his left foot in the stirrup, and swung his body seventeen hands up and onto Cowboy's back.

The Tennessee walker quickened at the nudge of knees, and they galloped across low Needlegrass and patches of Birchleaf buckthorn. Once past a thicket of juniper, Arizona cypress, and several regional Madrone trees, Barrett slowed the horse to climb higher onto a trail through Ponderosa pine and Douglas fir. He guided Cowboy cautiously through a shallow stand of golden-leafed aspen and into a clearing where a galvanized water tank was positioned next to a windmill.

Barrett dismounted by the open tank, and he and Cowboy drank deeply. Scraps jumped paws up on the tank rim to dip her tongue and lap, lap, lap. She laid down in the sunshine with her sides heaving and her tongue hanging out, panting.

Barrett stood hands on hips and looked around at the surrounding Davis Mountains. Mount Livermore rose more than eight thousand feet to the south. The mountains had formed during the Cenozoic volcanoes era. They had built up over several million years and were radically different from the limestone plateaus and mountains of Big Bend National Park near the Rio Grande.

Barrett slung his worn boots forward through sparse clumps of yellow Deergrass toward a spot of scrub oak. He kicked away small rocks, took off his hat, and fell to his knees, mindless of small, hard points.

"Dear Lord," he began with his face lifted skyward. "I'm more entangled than that calf. Help me get loose, and I won't get in this mess ag'in."

He lowered his head and thought of what he'd told his son: *All a man has in this life is his word, his reputation. Will my son want to be like me now?*

He bowed his head in remorseful silence for several minutes. Vowing to set things right, he leaped up, jammed on his hat, and spun toward Cowboy and Scraps.

"Come on, partners! Let's go home." He let out a whoop, swung up, and nudged Cowboy to a run toward home.

* * *

Jane gathered eggs from the henhouse and headed to the kitchen with the handle of the wicker basket over her arm. She stopped at the sound of hoofbeats and saw Barrett riding up to the corral.

He pulled his horse up near her with his eyes beamed on hers.

"Good morning." He watched her anxious face change into a radiant smile. "I need to talk to you."

He slid from the saddle and reached for her. She set the basket down and held her arms out. He clutched her outstretched hands, never taking his eyes from hers as he told her all that had happened with Sam.

"I was so stupid, Jane! Can you forgive me?"

She put her arms around him and pressed her head into his chest.

"I love you, Barrett," she whispered as tears slid down her face.

"I'm ready to set things straight—take whatever is comin' to me. Let's go into town and talk to the sheriff, or maybe Frank's boss."

Jane raised her head, nodding and dabbing wet cheeks. She carried the eggs into the house while Barrett removed Cowboy's saddle and bridle, brushed him down quickly, poured a bucket of oats into the feeding trough, and checked his water supply.

He rushed into the house where he showered, shaved, and dressed. He stepped sock footed to find his good boots in the hall closet and sat on a kitchen chair to pull them on. Grabbing his best hat and jacket from hooks by the back door, he pushed out, letting the screen door slam behind him. Jane quickly gathered her purse and shawl and followed her husband.

"I'll call Sam and let him know what I aim to do," he said, lifting his cellular phone from the truck seat. "I owe him that. What he does about it is his own business."

"What's up?" drawled Sam.

"Are you in Alpine?" Barrett asked.

"Sure thing," Sam replied.

"Sam, I'm comin' clean. Comin' into town now to the Highway Patrol office to let them know about us. It's about an hour's drive for me. If you wanna meet me there, fine. If not—your choice."

"Whaddaya mean?" Sam yelled into his cell phone. "Meet you there? Have you lost your ever-lovin' mind?"

Barrett clicked his phone off.

* * *

Within the hour, a clean-shaven, slick-combed Sam Bassinger showed up at the Highway Patrol office and asked at the front desk if he might speak with Captain Butler.

"Please have a seat," the young officer at the front desk replied. He picked up a telephone. "What's your name?"

"Bassinger. Sam Bassinger," he answered, removing his hat.

"The judge's son?"

"Yeah."

"Sam! I know you." Surprise was written all over the young man's face as he chuckled. "You clean up real nice."

Sam ignored him, looking down the hallway. "Son of a bitch!" he muttered under his breath as he took a seat in the waiting area.

He saw Butler walk from a back office into the long hall. They made eye contact, and Butler motioned with his hand. "Come on back, Sam."

They shook hands in his office.

"Bill Butler. How can I help you?"

"Sam Bassinger."

Sam looked at the captain and averted his eyes. "My friend Barrett Compton will be here any minute," he blurted. "We have some information for you. Wanted to try and help you with this murder investigation."

"Murder?" Butler stood behind his desk with his eyes steady on Sam. "Does this have to do with Frank Johnson?"

"Yes, sir." Sam nodded and placed his hands on his hips, staring defiantly at the captain.

"Any murder investigation within Brewster County is handled by Ranger Trent and Sheriff Carlton."

Sam realized that the captain was watching him closely. He felt unsure with this change thrown at him. "So should we talk to one of them first?"

"Right." Butler sat down. "Have a seat. The sheriff's in town today, at his office. Do you know where it is?"

"Yeah, I reckon." Sam drew an audible breath, ignoring the invitation to sit. "Can I wait here for my buddy?" He began to crack his knuckles and pace the floor. He felt Butler's eyes on him.

"Would you like me to go to the sheriff's office with you, Sam?"

Sam stopped pacing. "I wish you would, sir."

The phone rang on Butler's desk. "Excuse me while I get this." He looked back at Sam. "I'll meet you there."

Butler picked up the phone and swiveled his chair around, his back to Sam as he talked.

Sam stepped out into the hallway to wait for Barrett.

* * *

As Barrett and Jane drove toward Alpine, he thought of that fateful night. How Sam's long-bed pickup had eased along a narrow asphalt road from Big Bend National Park toward Marathon in the hours before dawn. The truck had bumped heavily over those double railroad tracks that paralleled the highway, its cargo lifting, shifting, and settling again with a clunk.

He had sat silently on the cab seat in the shadows as Sam braked at the stop sign. The single light pole cast an eerie glow on Sam's face as he opened a window to the heavy scent of sage and creosote bush, and thumped a cigarette butt into yellow haze. Sweat trickled down his face and dripped from his chin, despite the chilled air.

"No highway patrol in sight," Sam muttered.

They turned left onto Highway 90. It was an arrow shot through the isolated strip of Marathon, a former train stop called the gateway to Big Bend National Park. Faint outlines of the old Gage Hotel loomed ghostlike under shrouded starlight.

Sam held the pickup to a moderate speed as they drove west into early winter wind, fog, and drizzle. The swish-click, swish-click of the windshield wipers tapped a rhythm far too slow for Barrett's racing heart. Just then, Barrett lurched forward, startling Sam.

"Over there! On the right! See the rig?"

An eighteen-wheeler truck was parked off the highway, barely visible but for its parking lights—like little eyes glowing red in the gloom.

"Barrett!"

Jane's voice jarred him from his disturbing memories. They had arrived in Alpine, and Jane was calling him out of the past. He turned and drove to the Texas Highway Patrol office. He and Jane entered the building to find Sam waiting in the hallway.

The two men eyed one another for a moment.

Sam tossed his head toward the door. "He said for us to go see the sheriff."

* * *

"I need a strategy for landing the job as head of my department," Doris told Katherine that afternoon on her office phone. "Bruce Todd wants that position too."

"Does he have as many qualifications as you?" Katherine asked.

"No," Doris answered and pushed her chair back from her desk. "But he was born with an edge—being male. You know, Katherine—as all women know—we have to be twice as good to be good enough to get the job."

"They say dress for success. That's what all the how-to books say," Katherine advised.

"That pains me," Doris said with a sigh. "You know how I love loose skirts and blouses in bright, gypsy colors."

A light knock sounded. Doris looked up to see Sandy Wisner standing in her doorway, smiling. "Come in," she said, motioning him inside.

"Katherine, I have a visitor. I'll call later." Doris hung up the phone and fanned herself with a folder in the suddenly warm room.

The lean and debonair young man walked toward her. Doris stretched her hand forward to greet him and bumped a half-filled can of Diet

Coke, which tumbled brown liquid across the papers scattered on her desk.

"Let me help," Sandy said. He pulled a large, white handkerchief from a back trouser pocket and mopped the desktop.

Doris grabbed Kleenex, and together they sopped up wet papers and daubed the desk. Looking up to meet one another's eyes, they began laughing.

"I hope you know that you have an admirer," Sandy said with a wink.

Doris lost her smile and lowered her eyes.

"May I treat you to a glass of wine or a cocktail downtown?" he asked tentatively.

There was an awkward silence.

"Yes," she finally answered. "Yes. That would be nice. Thank you."

"How about Zeppie's?"

"I'll meet you there."

She left everything just as it was, locked the door behind her, and followed Sandy out of the building.

* * *

Katherine tossed restlessly most of the night, awaiting the morning light. She'd called Captain Butler that evening and left a message, eager to find out more about the people she'd seen earlier. There had been no response.

She felt the need to be involved in the here and now, and this investigation with Doris might be a way for that. But it was as if she were living in two worlds: the past, and now a prospect of something different. Her pain was ever present. As hard as she tried to suppress her memories, they kept popping up at odd moments. *Maybe I need to see a shrink.*

Around three in the morning, she finally fell asleep.

She walked along a shaded pathway carrying Bananas in her arms. She saw a rope swing with a wooden seat that held a slender young woman humming sweetly as she dipped her feet, moving to and fro.

Katherine approached the swing, and Maureen dragged her feet to a stop, leaned back, and looked up at her mother. Bananas licked the girl's face.

Katherine looked into her daughter's eyes and whispered, "I love you."

"I know, Mom."

Bananas snorted at the foot of the bed, and Katherine edged toward wakefulness.

She gazed into bright white light and watched as thin, clear glass in the shape of a heart glided forcefully past her as if on a string, crashing into a rock wall. Millions of fractures appeared, yet somehow the heart held together.

Bananas snored loud enough to rouse her slightly. She tossed and turned over on her side in the soft, queen-sized bed.

She sat in a tiny grocery store and bar, knowing it to be a shop along a narrow, cobbled lane in Venice. Open bins held salami and cheeses next to fruit and vegetables next to refrigerated cases filled with bottled drinks. People sat around her at small tables and spoke in low voices over coffee, beer, or wine. Rain drizzled onto the windows, enclosing the cozy space. The front door opened, and her head jerked toward it, her heart soaring with joy.

She awoke with a start and sat up in bed. Sadness stilled her heart. It was but a dream. Brann was not meeting her.

She held both hands to her head, raking her hair back and sobbing. "I must stop waiting for him! He's never coming back. I have to either leave it or get on with life."

CHAPTER SEVEN

After coffee the next morning, Katherine told Bananas, "Action! I must stop waiting for things to happen and do something."

She called the Highway Patrol office from her kitchen phone and asked for Captain Butler.

"Hello, Ms. Bell," Butler said. "Sorry to keep you waiting. I'm in a meeting just now. Can this wait until after lunch?"

"But I told you that I *saw* the kidnappers!" she exclaimed.

"This is about those neighbors you told me about?"

"Yes, it is."

"If you feel it's that urgent, you might want to call the local police. I'm sorry, but I'm tied up for a couple of hours with this murder investigation. I can check back with you then."

She covered the phone's receiver tightly with her hand, threw her head back, and moaned, "Of course it's urgent! That's why we talked on Sunday morning!"

"Ms. Bell?"

She removed her hand from the mouthpiece.

"All right, thank you."

Katherine wailed aloud as she hung up the phone, "A couple of *hours!*"

She looked at Bananas napping in front of the oven.

"Anything could have happened up there."

Bananas lifted her head, listening.

Katherine dialed her brother's cell phone. Busy.

She pressed the digits of another number and spoke to an answering machine. "Doris, call me as soon as possible! I'm at home."

She looked glumly at Bananas, who had nodded off again.

"This is the day Doris teaches from nine until four, the day she has only ten-minute breaks. She can't just drop everything and run over here."

Bananas opened one eye and looked at her.

Katherine frowned and said, "In fact, no one we know can do that; they all hold steady jobs. I'm the only one not working. Who'd want a zombie around anyway?"

Bananas got up and came to her side.

Katherine patted her soft fur and then pressed Susanna's phone number.

"This is Susanna. I'm substitute teaching in Marfa today. Leave a message."

The house on the hill was visible from where she stood by the kitchen phone. Katherine gazed at it and thought of *Wuthering Heights* and tortured souls.

She grasped the phone again, punched in a nine and a one, and halted. What would she tell the police? That she'd never actually *seen* these neighbors except as shadows behind the tinted windows of a car, but that she *believed* they'd been taken hostage?

She felt herself flush. Would the police do any more than laugh at her? Even her brother thought she might be making a mountain out of a molehill.

"But I have to do *something*," she explained to Bananas, who was standing by her water bowl, ears pricked forward, tail twitching.

"You and I will go." Katherine grabbed a leash from the backroom closet with Bananas close on her heels.

Katherine snapped the leash to Bananas's leather collar. "I'll take my cell phone, and we'll be very careful. If we see anything odd, we'll run."

They went out the door and through the gate at the rear of her yard.

* * *

Susanna tried to keep the fourth-graders quiet and orderly as they entered the school cafeteria for lunch. Little chance. They were hungry and primal with growling stomachs. They ran, pushed, and squealed.

Susanna thought of how Lisa and Clay woke up grumpy every school morning. She didn't like her role as drill sergeant, yelling out the routine so they could get to school on time. *And this is even more hectic!*

"Ms. Perez?" a small voice interrupted.

She looked down at a scrawny little boy tugging on her pants leg and rubbing tears and a runny nose.

"Yes, Pablo," she answered.

Now I have snot on my pants leg!

"Felicia has my shoe and won't give it back," he sobbed.

"*Where* is Felicia?"

Pablo pointed across the cafeteria to a group of little girls huddled at a table, giggling and wiggling in waves like Jell-O.

"Come with me." Susanna marched across the room, and Pablo followed.

She stood glaring over the girls until the shoe was meekly handed up. She returned it to Pablo just as the bell rang.

Kay Taylor Burnett

Now she could take her lunch break, all twenty minutes of it.

"Well, hell-o," said a deep-throated voice inside the teacher's lounge. Mary Bassinger turned toward the door wearing a tight sweater, short skirt, and high-heeled shoes. A glittering bracelet caressed her ankle, and her long earrings clinked when she moved.

Susanna smiled, thinking that Mary looked more like an aging hooker than a full-time high school English teacher.

Enrollment was small at the 1A school; elementary, middle, and high school classes were held in separate buildings on the same campus, and the teachers shared a lounge. Susanna sat at a pale green, Formica-topped table, opened her brown-bag lunch, and watched Mary pick at raw veggies and sip a diet cola.

Like she needs to lose weight?

Next to Mary sat Kelly Krimshaw, elementary principal, who also taught various grades when needed.

"How do you do it?" Susanna rumpled her face and stared at her sandwich.

"Do what?" Mary looked perplexed.

"This! Teach school every day," Susanna groaned. "I just substitute, so I have a real life away from here."

"Oh, there are a lot worse jobs than this," Mary said, tossing her mane of tinted red hair over a shoulder. "And I just fall in *love* with my students every year."

Let's hope she's not serious, Susanna thought. "How about you, Kelly?"

Kelly looked up and shrugged. "It beats living fifty miles out on a ranch." She neatly folded her sandwich wrapper and placed it next to her bottled water.

Kelly was dressed in a conservative navy wool suit, crisp white blouse, and pumps. She wore her glossy brown hair in a well-cut bob pulled behind her ears, showing off her pearl earrings.

"You live on a ranch?" Susanna asked.

"I grew up on one; no one around for miles. Shootin' prairie dogs for entertainment."

Susanna cringed at the thought of those cute, little critters standing sentry by their earthly homes and Kelly raising a straight arm to fire a shot through their small, furry heads.

She laid her head down onto her cradled arms resting on the table. "I've been running a *plant* nursery, away from teaching too long, I guess," she moaned. *And lacking the strength needed for a class full of elementary school–aged kids.*

"Are you going to the Friday night football game?" Mary looked into her compact mirror and applied a fresh coat of shiny lipstick as Susanna raised her head.

"Me? I wouldn't dare. Lisa and Clay would never forgive me," she answered, sitting upright.

"Oh, that's right." Mary returned the compact to her purse. "I forgot that you have children in Alpine schools. The rivalry is unbelievable! But honey, they aren't playing Alpine, and it's a good place to meet single guys." Her glistening lips widened into a smile, and she winked at Kelly.

"Ha!" Kelly responded. "Men are as scarce as antlers durin' huntin' season around here."

Susanna looked back to Mary. "Do you live in Marfa?"

"Oh no," Mary said. "Harlan and I have lived in Alpine for the last twenty years. He's a district judge, you know, and busy, too busy." She pursed her lips in a theatrical pout.

Susanna abruptly thought of checking her phone messages. "Excuse me." She stood and crossed the room, pulling a cell phone from her pocket and pressing the On button.

There were two messages. "Susanna, Bill Butler here. Could I interest you in attending a Friday night football game with me? Call me, please." He gave a phone number in warm, friendly tones. The second was from Katherine—cryptic in tone. "Call me! As soon as possible!"

Mary buttoned a gray smock (recommended by the principal, Susanna suspected) over the tight sweater and short skirt to return to the classroom. She rose and picked up her paper wrappings and drink can. "Is that Captain Bill Butler with the Highway Patrol?"

Susanna felt the blood rush to her face. *God, she listened!*

"Big, handsome man," Mary said with a grin, sliding her trash into a tall garbage can. "Big hands, big feet ..."

The school bell rang.

"Saved by the bell." Susanna laughed, rushing back to her classroom.

* * *

Katherine restrained Bananas on the leash as they climbed up the steep, dirt road behind her house. She wished that she'd taken the time to change into hiking boots or tennis shoes. Bananas tugged at the lead, as if reminding her that time was of the essence.

Again, the driveway gate was open.

"Maybe there's no one home," she whispered to Bananas. She remembered years ago when she had hitched a ride into Fort Davis for gas with that family from Presidio. "Things are seldom what they seem," she said, mustering the courage to go on.

She shortened Bananas's leash and continued up the drive, stopping to check the open garage for the license plate number of that sports car. The Burksons' black sedan sat in one stall; she wrote the license number on a small pad from her pocket. The green sports car filled another space.

She wrote down its make and description, along with the license number.

"So, are the kidnappers here?" she quizzed Bananas. "They could be murderers, too. Frank Johnson was murdered the night this car passed us at breakneck speed."

She shivered and moved into the shallow shade of a maple tree losing its leaves next to the garage. She flipped open her cell phone—no signal. She shook the phone and tried again with the same result.

Bananas cocked her head and barked.

"Sssshhh! We've come this far," Katherine whispered. "It will only take a minute more. We'll just ring the doorbell and scoot back down the hill. Just knowing someone's around might be enough to scare them off."

Bananas gurgled but didn't pull back as they crept up the walk, mounted a narrow concrete step, and crossed the low porch. Katherine stood at arm's length from the broad double doors and stretched a trembling finger toward the doorbell. She pressed the button and heard chimes sound within the house. Then she heard footsteps clapping on a marble floor. The steps grew louder, and then stopped. The door slowly cracked. A muscular young man wearing a black T-shirt and blue jeans stood in the gap.

Katherine gasped. *It was the same man who had driven the car full of strangers past her house!*

Straight black hair hung forward over a narrow, gaunt face. Katherine chilled as piercing blue eyes held hers.

"I, I came to see the Burksons," she stammered.

"Come in." The young man's face was solemn.

Bananas bristled.

He looked down at the dog, opening the door just wide enough for them to enter.

"Uh. No, thank you," she said as she began to back away. "If they're busy, I can come another time." She gathered Bananas's leash and prepared to run.

A strong hand caught her arm, causing Katherine to squeak in surprise.

"But I insist," the man said. "Come in."

* * *

Doris was getting worried. She had returned Katherine's call during the morning break and again when morning classes ended.

Where could Katherine be after leaving that breathless message?

She called the listed number for Ambrose Trent in Fort Davis. No answer. She checked for the number of the Highway Patrol office, called, and asked for Captain Butler, waiting for him to pick up the call.

"Captain Butler?" Doris identified herself as Katherine's friend, told him about the message she had received that morning from Katherine, and explained that she had not been able to reach Katherine since.

"I think she went up to that house."

"And you think she might be in danger?" he asked, recalling the Sunday morning conversation with Katherine and Susanna. They had been very concerned.

"I don't know what to think, but I'm going to Katherine's. If she's not there, I'm going up to that house," Doris said.

"Don't go alone," he warned.

Susanna might end a relationship before it ever has a chance to get started if I don't check on her friends. And who knows; it might merit investigation. Stranger things have happened.

"I can meet you there within the hour," Butler said.

"Thank you," Doris said. "I'll be waiting at Katherine's back door."

Butler knew the rules. A Texas Ranger had first priority in matters of federal law, then the local sheriff, and then the police. It was a long shot, but this *could* be connected to Frank Johnson's death. At least the ladies seemed more than a little unnerved. And he sure wanted to look good to Susanna.

Butler dialed a number and switched his phone to speaker at his office desk. "Hey, Trent. What's new on the Johnson case?"

"Butler! Good to hear from you. Yeah, Sheriff Carlton called me over to meet with those local guys you sent to his office. Now we have a description of the men driving that eighteen-wheeler. Do you have time to get together today?"

"Sure. What time?" Butler swiveled his chair around to view the big clock on his office wall.

"Anytime." Trent sounded casual.

"I'd like to hear about it. Can you stop by now?" Butler thumbed through recent messages that had been left on his desk. "I'd appreciate it if you could check on a separate situation with me that may or may not be connected to the murder."

"Sure thing. I'll be there in about twenty minutes."

Butler sighed with relief. *There might be nothing going on at that Burkson house, but just in case, it would be best to have Ranger Trent along. Better call Carlton too.*

"Sheriff? This is Captain Butler, Texas Highway Patrol." He clicked on the telephone speaker.

"What can I do you for, Cap?"

Butler explained to the sheriff that he was making a house call as a personal favor and that Ranger Trent would be with him. He jotted a note on his calendar of the proposed visit and took time to freshen up in the men's room before grabbing his hat and heading out to his car.

Trent arrived within minutes and parked next to Butler's car. As they shook hands Butler asked, "What's the latest on Johnson's murder?"

Trent chuckled and got into Butler's patrol car. "Those fellas, Bassinger and Compton, are singing like canaries about stealing plants from the park."

Trent flicked ashes from the short stub of a smoldering cigar out his window as they drove toward Katherine Bell's house. "They gave statements about being at the crime scene and descriptions of the truckers. The sheriff forwarded the information to the Dallas office where composite drawings of the suspects will be made and posted."

"How did they know who was at that spot?" Butler puzzled. "I'm trying to get the connection with Sam and Barrett."

"Well, it gets a little complicated there," the ranger said as he pulled a side seat lever, pushing the seat all the way back. He stretched his stovepipe boots forward on the floorboard and explained, "Bassinger is a wily fella and the son of District Judge Harlan Bassinger."

He paused to puff the remains of the fat stub, its glow ebbing.

"Bassinger asked for immunity from prosecution in exchange for information," he continued. "Seems they had a rendezvous with the truck drivers. It's clear that the two men *were* at the murder scene; 'before it happened,' they claim. So the sheriff called the DA about a possible plea bargain for both."

He gave up on the cigar, snubbed it between his thumb and index finger, and dropped it out the window. "That doesn't eliminate either as a suspect, and their information gives us somethin' to go on."

Butler nodded his understanding and signaled a right turn. "And the tire treads?"

"We've been working on those tire treads," Trent said, patting his shirt pockets in search of a fresh smoke. "Seems that a fourth vehicle stopped at that site—a car other than the eighteen-wheeler, Bassinger's truck, and Johnson's patrol car."

He pulled the wrapper from a new cigar and lit it.

"Do you have the probable make of it from those treads?" Butler asked as he slowed near Katherine's back driveway.

"Yep. A small car, most likely foreign made," Trent answered as they pulled up and stopped behind Katherine's SUV. "This is my sister's house," he said with surprise.

"Right," Butler said. "I got a call from her friend who's worried about Katherine."

Doris heard car doors slamming and pushed the iron gate open with her wooden staff as the officers walked toward it.

Not one officer, but two. Katherine's brother, the ranger! So, they think this is serious too.

"She isn't here!" Doris spoke directly to Ranger Trent. "And neither is her dog. I think she's up at that house." Doris pointed her walking stick at the house on Hancock Hill.

Trent turned on his boot heel and headed back to the patrol car.

"Do you want to wait here while we check?" Butler asked Doris.

Doris began striding out the gate. "Heck, no. I'm coming with you!"

The twosome caught up with the ranger near the car. Trent opened the back door for Doris.

"Does my cigar bother you, ma'am?" Trent held up a brightly burning cigar, and she noticed his face was drawn with worry lines.

"Not if the windows are open." *Nasty habit*, she thought as she crawled in and opened wide her window.

They backed out of the driveway and spun forward up the street, turning left on the dirt road behind Katherine's house. The bumps in the road jostled Doris on the backseat, and she choked on the dust swirling through the window. It was chilly with the window open, so she pulled her red, woolen cloak up around her ears.

A forlorn train whistle echoed from downtown. *Sinister sound. I hope it's not an omen.*

The neighbor's driveway gate was open, and Butler drove through to the entrance near the back of the house.

"Wait here!" Trent said to Doris, who flinched at the gruff command.

She restrained herself as Butler and Trent got out of the vehicle and walked up to the double doors. She had to admit they looked impressive—two tall men in boots, Stetson hats, and jackets open to reveal guns flashing at their hips.

Trent rang the doorbell as Butler held a position alongside the porch, scanning the terrain. After a moment, they heard a dog yowling inside as if tigers were at the door.

Doris recognized Bananas's bark and quickly got out of the car, shuffling on her cane up behind Captain Butler to see what was happening.

A lean young man wearing a T-shirt with "One Way" printed over a finger pointing upward opened the door, and a small dog arched in the gap, every yelp lifting her body into the air.

"Bananas! Come here!" Katherine rushed forward. "Hush!"

The dog stopped yapping and wagged her tail as Katherine scooped her up from the doorway.

"I'm sorry," Katherine said rising. She cradled Bananas in the doorway. "Oh, hello, Ambrose, Captain Butler."

Trent quickly assessed his sister as Doris hollered from behind, "Katherine! Are you all right?"

Katherine didn't look at her but down at Bananas and smiled. "Yes. Of course."

Doris thought her smile guarded.

The young man questioned, "Is this official?" His eyebrows squeezed together in a serious, angular face.

"May we come in?" Ranger Trent boomed.

The young man's eyes narrowed as he asked, "What's this about?" He opened the door a little wider.

Trent and Butler filed through the doorway with Doris close behind.

In flowing movement, the ranger squinted again at Katherine and removed his hat with the same hand that held a cigar curled under his index finger, saying, "Texas Ranger Ambrose Trent."

"Horace James," the young man said with an audible gulp.

Butler removed his hat and stretched a hand forward to the stranger. "Captain Bill Butler, Texas Highway Patrol."

The glum expression never left the young man's face as he tentatively offered his hand in return.

Trent focused intensely on Katherine as she held Bananas closely. She met his gaze without comment.

"Come in," the young man said and turned to lead the group down the hallway.

Katherine stooped and slowly released the dog on the floor. As she rose, Doris gave her a searching look and whispered, "Are you all right?"

Katherine's eyes followed Bananas. "Of course."

The women trailed the men along the hallway, through a wide arched doorway, and into a large, formal room. Oriental rugs graced wooden parquet floors; expensive furniture and paintings decorated the expansive walls of a high ceiling room. An entire wall of windows gave a panoramic view of the small town of Alpine nestled in a valley and the mountains beyond. At one end of the long room, an enormous fireplace blazed with burning logs.

An elderly couple huddled close together on a sofa near the fire, a soft pastel throw spread over their knees.

Doris wondered if their hands were handcuffed or tied beneath the blanket. She smiled at the couple. They inclined their heads but didn't speak. *Had they been warned not to?*

She cut her eyes toward the young man who said his name was Horace. He wore his shirttail out and hanging loose. *Was that to hide a gun?* Three other people, two women and a man, were sitting quietly near the windows. She studied them for a clue as to who they might be.

Doris shifted her eyes back to the lawmen. *Were they aware that these people might be armed? No, Butler seems to be studying a portrait beside the doorway. Trent is just looking around the room.*

"Is there someplace I can put this thing?" The ranger held his burning cigar at arm's length.

Doris took a deep breath. *Why hadn't these people been more surprised to see law officers here?*

The old woman frowned and gestured toward a crystal ashtray on an oriental, mother-of-pearl inlaid coffee table.

"Thank you, ma'am." The ranger stepped forward, extinguished his cigar, and glanced back at the fragile woman. Her sallow face showed no emotion.

There was an awkward moment of silence.

Doris was wary that Katherine hadn't introduced the people in the room. Her attention seemed glued on Bananas.

"I'm Doris Kemp," said the professor, extending her hand to the young man, her eyes zooming back to the elderly couple.

He took her hand and nodded toward the old man. "This is my Uncle Jake and Aunt Gladys Burkson."

He dropped Doris's hand, nodded toward the lawmen, and turned to speak to the old couple. "This is Texas Highway Patrol Captain Butler and

Texas Ranger Trent. I believe the ranger is related to your neighbor, Mrs. Bell."

The lawmen turned to the Burksons, who looked blank.

Oh my God. They're terrified! Doris thought.

"And these," Katherine interjected, walking behind Doris and waving her hand toward the people seated at a small game table in front of the window, "are Horace's friends, or I should say Race, as he prefers to be called."

She nodded at each. "Meet Janis, Ellie, and Frank from Chicago."

Chicago! The mob! Doris flinched.

The young women, clad in blue jeans and loose shirts, tilted their heads and smiled. A youthful, middle-aged man rose and said, "Hello."

Doris watched carefully. *Who are these people? Are they as harmless as they look? Katherine called the young man Race. Sounds like a gang name.*

"Please, have a seat," Race said and showed Doris to a wingback chair in dark patterns of cut velvet, while the lawmen sat in matching leather chairs trimmed with big brass buttons.

Doris scrutinized Katherine's move to a soft, teal-colored sofa opposite the elderly couple where she eased into matching feather pillows. Bananas laid across her feet.

Was the dog relaxed? No! Doris decided that she was protecting Katherine.

One of the young women rose from her chair. "May we serve you a drink? We have coffee, tea, soft drinks, or water."

Oh my God, here it comes: drugs! "Water, please," Doris said in a tight voice. *At least water was clear.* "Thank you."

Trent and Butler exchanged glances. "I'd sure appreciate a cup of coffee," said the ranger.

Butler nodded. "The same, please; black."

Doris watched the man at the table follow the two women out of the room. *It doesn't take three people to serve coffee. What are they planning?* She wished for a handful of extra-strength Advil to take for her headache.

"Please call me Race. My friends do. Mrs. Bell told us earlier of your concerns about … about Uncle Jake," Race began. "And about my sports car, which was nowhere near the highway on the night she drove from Houston back to Alpine."

Uh-oh, thought Doris, *they know she's on to them.*

"Where do I begin?" Race looked down, his eyebrows knit together.

"You might start with my calling you in Chicago," Mr. Burkson said in a quivering voice. He placed a gnarled hand gently over his wife's atop the soft blanket.

"Right," Race said, moving toward the huge fireplace. "Uncle Jake called me in Chicago. As you may know, he and my aunt moved from

Houston to Alpine some years ago to retire. They don't have computers, so they don't e-mail, but we've stayed in touch by letters and phone calls. I knew their activities had lessened, but they hadn't mention how restricted they'd become."

The young women returned from the kitchen with trays laden with water, coffee, and cups of hot tea for the Burksons.

Race sat down on the sofa near Katherine.

For a few moments it was quiet but for the tinkle of china and silver and the crackle of logs in the fireplace.

Race heaped sugar and cream into his coffee and stirred before taking a gulp. He drew a deep breath. "Uncle Jake and Aunt Gladys took me in after my parents died in a car accident in Austin when I was a freshman in high school. When I graduated from U of C this June, I'd hoped they'd be there." He smiled at his uncle.

"I don't see well enough to drive anymore," Jake Burkson said in a loud, shaking voice. "Can't hear much either." He chuckled as he looked at his wife. "Fact is, neither of us can hear a damn thing."

"He told me that they were failing in health," Race said, "and asked if I could come to Alpine and drive them to Houston and settle them into assisted-living quarters." He stood and stoked the fire, placing another log on it.

The room was silent. Doris felt her head and breathing return to normal as she waited for him to continue.

"And I told him this house would be all his," Jake Burkson announced. "Too big for us now and too cold in the winter." He turned to Gladys, who nodded stiffly in agreement.

Race addressed the guests as he paced in front of the fireplace. "I joined a singles prayer group in Chicago. Frank, Ellie, and Janis are in that group." He smiled at his friends who had returned to sit at the small table by the windows. "As global wars escalate and scandals of corruption shake the nation, we've been praying for God's direction. When that huge hurricane hit; another massacre devastated a college campus; and the threat of economic collapse became imminent, we believed that God's judgment was close at hand."

He nodded toward his friends. "Several of us had asked specifically for a place of refuge and service during the coming chaos. When Uncle Jake offered this place, Frank, Ellie, and Janis felt pressed to come with me to Alpine to await whatever's coming."

The room was still enough to hear Bananas's soft, rhythmic snoring.

The lawmen exchanged looks.

"Are you what they call 'survivalists'?" the ranger demanded.

Doris watched him fumble in his shirt pocket for a cigar and saw him halt, fingers mid-pocket, at a withering look from Mrs. Burkson.

"No, sir!" Race picked up his coffee cup from the low table. "We're not predicting the crash of the stock market nor a revolution in the U.S. We're simply waiting for God to reveal his plans for us."

The young woman named Ellie spoke. "My sister and I have believed for some time that major changes are happening in our world, and especially in this country."

"We're not troublemakers, sir," Frank said, looking steadily at the lawmen. "We just want to be where God wants us. We think that's here in Far West Texas. We hope to be of service in this community."

Butler got up and stood by the chair, rotating his hat in his hands. He looked at Race. "Well, I think that's all we need to hear for now. I wish you well. If I can be of help, please call me."

He reached into his shirt pocket, drew out a business card, and handed it to the young man.

The captain glanced over his shoulder. "Trent?"

Trent pulled his lower lip in, stood and put his hat on, nodded at the Burksons, and gave a lingering look at his sister. "Coming, Kath?"

She smiled and nodded. "I'll make my way back."

Butler walked over and stood before Doris with a questioning look. Doris returned his look over her round eyeglasses and smiled. She placed the full water glass on a small chest next to her chair and struggled to her feet. "Thank you, Captain Butler, for coming. I think I'll walk back with Katherine." She reached for her staff.

Butler nodded and followed Trent to the front entrance. Race trailed and stepped forward to open the massive door, saying, "Thank you for checking on my aunt and uncle."

"You're welcome," answered Butler and shook Race's hand in parting.

Katherine nudged Bananas and rose from the sofa. She stood close to the elderly couple, bending down close so they could hear her.

"Thank you for your kind hospitality."

Jake Burkson smiled, and his wife nodded primly.

"You have a fine nephew," Katherine added.

Doris watched the three at the small table rise and walk toward Katherine, who turned to them, saying, "I can only hope that you'll enjoy this region. As I said earlier, I live just down the mountainside, and I'm happy to have you as neighbors. You are welcome anytime. And please, call me Katherine."

The young women and Frank smiled and thanked her.

Doris had her stick in hand and moved toward the door with Katherine. Race met them in the archway after seeing the officers out. "Leaving so soon?"

"I've been here all afternoon," Katherine said. "And *worried sick* that Bananas would have an accident on one of your aunt's oriental rugs!"

Katherine and Doris walked down the hillside with Bananas on her leash.

"What do you think?" Doris asked.

Katherine smiled. "I think that this mystery is solved!"

They laughed together.

"But was it his sports car you saw? Remember? The morning of Frank Johnson's murder?" Doris pressed.

"I don't know," Katherine said.

In the patrol car, Trent turned to Butler with a frown. "Bunch of kooks! I hope they don't start some kind of cult or a commune up here." He lit a fresh cigar and aimed a burst of aromatic smoke at the ceiling.

"They seem like well-meaning folks to me," Butler responded casually as he backed the car around to head out the driveway. "I've seen all kinds in this line of work, like you, and these people don't worry me like some do."

"I say we keep an eye on 'em!" Trent growled.

* * *

Doris returned to her campus office just after dark. She parked in front of her building and hurried to the front doors, searching for keys to enter.

No need; the janitor was vacuuming the hallway, saw her at the locked glass doors, and moved to open one.

She still needed the keys to unlock her office and stood in the hallway fumbling for the right one when she heard a voice behind her.

"Good evening, Professor Kemp."

Doris whirled about to face the flashing white teeth of Sandy Wisner.

"Oh, you startled me," she said flustered.

"So sorry. Please, let me help you with that." He moved very close to her and reached out, holding her cold hand firmly while gently extracting the key ring. He singled a key with a yellow plastic jacket and asked, "Could it be this one?"

Perspiration beaded Doris's forehead. She hesitantly took her eyes from his face to look at the key he held high. "Uh, yes. That's my office key. But really ... I can do this."

"Of course you can." He had already turned the key in the lock and was pushing the door open. "Are you always so reluctant to allow a gentleman the pleasure of helping you?"

"I ..." she stammered and swallowed a hard lump in her throat. "Thank you, Sandy." She moved inside, and he followed.

"Are you working late?" she asked.

"I was just leaving the library when I saw you come in," he explained. "I've wanted to have a moment alone with you."

Doris's fingers lost feeling, and the folder in her hand dropped with a thud to the floor. She clumsily bent down to retrieve it, as he, far quicker, stooped to get it for her, his warm breath meeting her face.

They straightened together. Doris stiffened.

He handed her the folder, saying, "Would you care to join me for a cocktail at Zeppie's?"

Doris drew a deep breath. "Now?"

"Yes, if you will do me the honor." He smiled down at her.

They heard a thud in the hallway, and they simultaneously poked their heads out the doorway. The janitor met their stare and shrugged as he moved the big commercial vacuum apparatus away from a nearby door.

Doris had her wits about her now and turned briskly to Sandy. "Perhaps another time? I have work to catch up on this evening." She forced a smile of dismissal, always effective in the classroom.

"I look forward to it," he said softly and exited her office.

Doris watched him go and moved behind her desk, placing her hand on a wildly thumping heart. She slapped her face with both hands and shook her head.

"I must be dreaming!"

CHAPTER EIGHT

Doris and Katherine sat quietly at a table near the frosty front windows of the Sixth Street Bakery, watching falling snow cover the deserted street out front.

"I've had no words, no voice, in these two years since Brann's death," Katherine said softly. "Silence has filled my days … my nights … my life." She paused and circled the rim of her teacup with an index finger. "And now that the silence is past, or could be, I have no one to talk to."

"You can talk to me," Doris said lightly, setting her cup on the table. She grew serious; "It can be a nightmare, Katherine, trapped in painful memories. But, it takes *time*, perhaps years, to discover anew who you are—separate from the intimacy and oneness in a long-term marriage."

"Time is still polishing the pyramids," Katherine quipped. "Intimacy? We could've lived on a piano wire." She sighed. "Being with Brann was like being by myself *with* someone. It was that comfortable."

Silence.

"And now," Katherine began again. "Now I feel *invisible*, even to myself. There's no one to confirm my existence by sharing the trivia of life. No one to protect me, especially from myself."

Her shoulders felt heavy. She drew and expelled a breath. She recalled seeing a statue called *Grief*. It was a sexless human figure dressed in a hooded cloak, the face absolutely emotionless— no sorrow, no joy.

"But," responded Doris with a weak smile, "at least you've reached a point of being able to talk about it."

The women sipped their tea. The room was quiet as the two widows stared through the café windows at the snowflakes fluttering in slow motion.

"Funny," Katherine murmured. "I thought that I understood the songs of Bob Dylan's youth, and mine, when he asked how it felt to be 'all alone' and 'on your own.' But I *hadn't* understood, not until now. The closer you are to someone, the more painful the separation."

She rose from the table and went to the coffee bar to pour more hot water for tea. She glanced back at Doris. "Want some?"

Doris shook her head.

Seated again at the table, Katherine leaned toward the frosted window next to her and rubbed two small circles on the glass, staring through each.

Doris thoughtfully watched her and said, "There are two kinds of widows, Katherine. Those who manage to get on with their lives and look for someone else, and those who say, 'This is it.' Of course loneliness and loss are not unique; life is perfectly fair. Heartbreak and disappointment come to one and all."

A clatter of dishes from the kitchen reminded them that they were not by themselves.

"How then should we live?" Katherine asked, pushing herself around to the table again, looking straight at Doris. "Treading time as we do." She quoted Shakespeare: "Tomorrow, tomorrow, and tomorrow?"

"There is another point of view." Doris lifted her eyes from the teacup. "One could say, get a life; stop hanging on to memories, clinging to your grief."

Katherine acknowledged the logic. "Right. I realize how closed I am to almost everyone, and therefore they are to me. But, Doris, I would be different if I could."

"You are understandably traumatized. But even with Susanna and me, you talk of *we* this and *we* that. What did *you* want or like or yearn for?" Doris asked.

"All I ever truly wanted is sitting in the corner of my living room, in an urn," Katherine said wistfully.

Doris looked startled. "Brann's *ashes*?"

"Not his ashes, which are there, but Brann himself," Katherine said. "Although far from perfect, he cherished me, Doris, and he empowered me to be all that I wanted or yearned to be."

"Listen," Doris said, looking straight into Katherine's eyes. "Life is a choice. You can think on things of death, and that's where you're headed, or you can think on things of life. Needless to say, Katherine, you have a lot to live for, a lot to give. For God's sake, choose life."

The bell on the bakery door jangled.

They jerked their heads up. "It's Susanna!" Doris said. "I didn't think she'd make it for lunch in this snow."

"Hey, guys!" Susanna waved and closed the door. "Brrrrr." She pulled leather gloves from her hands. "Didn't know if y'all would be here on a day like this."

She looked back out the front windows. "Isn't it beautiful?"

They all smiled and watched the snow fall.

"Yes," Doris laughed. "It's magical."

"But isn't early October a little early for snow?" Katherine protested. "Neither of my previous winters in Alpine came this early."

"You never know in these mountains," Susanna said. "We could have Indian summer next week."

The bell clanged again. Ranger Trent, Sheriff Carlton, and Captain Butler pressed inside the front door and stamped snow from their heavy boots.

Ranger Trent looked over and tipped his hat. "Howdy, ladies. Are you staying warm in that house, Katherine?"

She nodded with a smile. "Good, good," he responded.

The men moved toward the far back corner of the room.

"Hello, Susanna." Butler's eyes held hers as she smiled back.

She felt heat rise to her face as Captain Butler singled her out.

"You could be home in front of a warm fireplace," he teased as he moved on to join his associates.

"Looks like they want privacy," Katherine whispered as she watched the men retreat.

"Not all of them," Doris said and looked at Susanna.

Susanna turned quickly to check the blackboard menu. "Let's order our soup."

The men chose a distant table and removed their thick, water-repellant jackets to drape over the backs of chairs. They took off their hats, shook off the moisture, and placed them on empty chairs.

After they were seated, Trent looked around the room and said, "It seems private enough in here." He clasped his hands and laid them on the table. "Who killed Frank Johnson, and why? We assume it was in the line of duty. But was it?"

"Most likely," Sheriff Carlton said. "A few months ago a patrolman was shot up in the Panhandle area. It was a remote place like Marathon is, the middle of nowhere.

"He'd noticed a car parked at a roadside park for a day or two and decided to check on it. Well, he walks toward this fella sittin' at the picnic table, and Bam! Bam! He's just blown away. Turns out when they found the killer, he was a fugitive from Oklahoma."

"Johnson was young, his first job," said the ranger. "He didn't have no enemies out here." He stopped searching his pockets when the sheriff pointed to a "No Smoking" sign. Drumming his long fingers on the table, he said, "Seems to me we oughta investigate his lifestyle, family, friends. After that, check on the men who came forward with information."

"It's in the works, like you asked," Sheriff Carlton said. "We got the composite drawings from Dallas of the two guys in the semi like you asked for, and my people are searching for a match in criminal files."

"How about the tire tracks?" Butler quizzed.

"Other than the eighteen-wheeler, we have Bassinger's pickup, Johnson's patrol car, and an unknown, small, probably foreign-made car," Carlton answered.

"You mean like a Toyota or Volkswagen? Or do you mean something more exotic?" Trent asked.

"Could be," answered Carlton.

The ranger leaned forward. "Did you check for tracks on the opposite side of the highway?"

Silence.

"Nope. Didn't think of it." The sheriff examined his fingernails.

CHAPTER NINE

Susanna thrust her hands deeper into the pockets of her navy wool coat and huddled close to Bill on the icy metal bleachers. If Friday night football was a religion in Texas, this stadium was its temple—cold and uncomfortable, where the prayers of half of the congregants would not be answered. The Class 1A Marfa Short Horns were behind 35 to 7, and miracles seemed unlikely tonight. Except the miracle of how she felt sitting beside this hunk. He was nothing like Marcos, and yet she felt every bit as safe and comfortable with him as with the man she'd loved from childhood and had lost in an instant.

Anxiety over the score fevered the pitch of stadium chants and cheers of parents, brothers, sisters, aunts, uncles, friends, band and pep squad members, teachers, and community supporters.

A whistle blew sudden and shrill in the cold, crisp air. Bill nudged her. "This is my favorite part of Marfa games. Keep your eyes on the team."

Susanna pulled her soft, maroon scarf up over her mouth to block the frigid air and watched the badly shaken Short Horn players toss their helmets to the ground. Several pulled their numbered jerseys up over their heads, jerked shoulder pads loose, and in a dead run closed in on the marching band assembling in the end zone.

"They look so little," she murmured.

Susanna realized how small her son Clay was and that he too would want to play football in high school.

"They're amazing," Bill said as he watched. "Gutsy little guys!"

She blinked back tears as she watched the players, still in cleats and scuffed pants, button ill-fitting band uniform jackets over undershirts. Then they snatched instruments from an off-field table. She noticed the cheerleaders were gathering instruments too.

She saw the star quarterback pick up a flute. *The great thing about small towns and small schools is that the kids get to participate in so many things.*

The band was in formation. Another whistle sliced the air, the tall drum major snapped the downbeat, and off they went down the field playing, "There'll Be a Hot Time in the Old Town Tonight."

The wind, brass, and percussion played loudly, if not perfectly, and the fans in the home bleachers roared their approval.

The halftime performance ended, and the cheerleaders went back to their place in front of the home stands. Marfa football players returned to don helmets, shoulder pads, and jerseys once again, and huddled with the coach and teammates. The players broke the huddle shouting "Woo! Woo! Woo!" clapping their hands, and raising their fists with fingers extended like horns. They raced onto the field for a second-half slaughter.

"What optimism," Susanna said softly over a lump in her throat. She thought about how Marcos had overcome being small and Hispanic to become a star football player in an overwhelmingly Anglo high school—the sheen of determination reflected in all of his accomplishments.

The ballgame ended, the Marfa crowd silent. Susanna stole a look at Bill when the final whistle sounded.

"Want another hot dog?" Bill grinned at her, eyes teasing.

"Heavens, no!" She laughed at his ridiculous question.

He put his arm around her and pulled her close to his side. "Like to have a drink at Ray's Bar?"

Susanna nodded and took his arm as they stepped down several bleacher steps. It felt good to lean on his strength.

"Susanna!"

Susanna stopped and turned to see her principal scrambling down the steps.

"How was your first Marfa game?" Kelly asked breathlessly. "And *who* is your friend?"

"Hello, Kelly." *She sure acts differently away from the schoolyard.* "I loved being here! This is Bill Butler. Bill, Kelly Krimshaw."

Kelly reached out a purple woolen mitten and looked coyly up at Bill.

"Nice to meet you, Miss Krimshaw," he said, his tone formal and courteous as he touched her mitten.

"You too," she said adoringly. "Are y'all going to Ray's Bar? Everybody does."

The words hung in the air.

"Maybe we'll see you there," Susanna answered with a tight smile, trying to hide how pissed-off she felt at Kelly's flirting with Bill.

She looked around at the man who was staring at Kelly a few steps above them and twisted back to Kelly. "Are you with Sam Bassinger?"

"I sure am." Kelly grinned and strutted back to Sam. "See you," she said, looking back over her shoulder at Bill.

Susanna pulled her scarf and long coat more tightly over her sweater and jeans as Bill caught her gloved hand. They matched steps with their boots clanking down the lower rows.

They found Bill's vehicle in the unpaved parking lot. He opened the passenger door, and Susanna settled into his car, loosening her scarf and wondering if her feelings were disloyal to Marcos. *I can't help how I feel*, she decided as she watched Bill walk around the car, slide inside, and fasten his seat belt.

"Kelly is the principal at Marfa where I substitute teach." Her teeth chattered, maybe because of the cold, but more likely from the quiver she felt at being with this man. She wondered if her pheromones were as alluring as his.

"So you're a teacher *too*?" Bill sounded impressed as he revved the engine and turned on the heater, waiting for both to warm.

"I taught elementary school until my daughter, Lisa, was born. I took her with me when she was a baby to Pioneer Plants and helped my husband with the business." She bit her lip. Maybe she shouldn't talk about Marcos.

"Which do you prefer?"

"The plant nursery." Susanna kept her eyes on his profile as he maneuvered out of the parking lot. Her response was honest. She taught because she needed the money. She realized then that straightforwardness was the only path she knew.

"I have enough teaching to do with my own kids." She removed her leather gloves. "And speaking of kids, do you mind if we head back to Alpine? I'll be glad to fix you a drink or a cup of coffee at my house."

"That sounds good," he said, turning toward the highway heading east to Alpine.

Both were quiet for the next few minutes.

"Did you enjoy the game?" she asked, breaking the silence.

"Of course." He looked around smiling. "Did you?"

"Yes! It's the first time I've been to a Marfa game. It was inspiring."

She paused, wondering if she would scare him off by saying more.

"And this is the first time I've been out with anyone since my husband died. I guess that's why I was so quiet driving over. I was nervous."

He reached over and clasped her hand in a gentle squeeze. "Thank you for doing me the honor. Are you still nervous?"

"No. I feel comfortable with you, Bill. And safe. Thank you for asking me."

He pulled his hand back to the wheel. His voice was soft. "Would you think me rude to ask how your husband died?"

"Not at all. We were coming back from Midland at night. A deer leaped in front of us, and we hit it full force. I was thrown against the door and out of the car, but only suffered cuts and bruises and a broken ankle. The deer crashed through the front windshield, and Marcos was killed instantly."

"I'm sorry, Susanna. How long ago?"

"Three years." She paused and looked down. "It seems an eternity."

It dawned on her that it was an eternity—past—and life went forward. It felt right and good.

They were silent.

"And you? How long were you married?" she asked.

"Fifteen years. I was working undercover assignments and gone more than I was at home. She had every right to want a better life than that."

"I'm sorry. It must have been tough on you—and your daughter, Clarissa."

"It was." She saw him wince. "It still is."

He unzipped his leather jacket and loosened the collar of a soft, blue plaid shirt.

"You two seem to have a special bond," Katherine ventured.

"Yes, I'm lucky. Clarissa remained loyal to me as her dad, even when her mother met someone new. And her mother was fair about visitation." His eyes crinkled with a smile. "Although it was rough at first, trying to think of things to say or do with a twelve-year-old daughter."

She drew a deep breath as Bill visibly relaxed. "I know what you mean. Clay is now ten years old and gets bored with Mom stuff."

The car was warm enough that Susanna unbuttoned her coat.

"Does he like to go hunting?" Bill asked.

"He's never been. My parents live on a ranch near Amarillo—great quail country. I've hunted quail since I was a kid, but haven't had time to take Clay. My dad suffered a stroke two years ago and is paralyzed on one side. Seems that these three years have raced by with me trying to get things sorted out."

"Understandable," he said gently.

She squirmed. "Let's talk about you. Where did you grow up?"

He looked around and answered calmly. "In the Hill Country near Austin."

"And did you always want to be an officer of the law?" She placed her back against the door so she had a full view of him at the wheel.

"Absolutely not!" he said. Noticing how she was seated, he clicked the automatic lock button.

"What does that mean?" She was surprised.

"I had a scholarship to Stanford University. My dream. That was near the end of the Vietnam War. I was drafted anyway and placed in Army Intelligence."

A quick calculation put him in his late forties, about ten or eleven years older than her. "So you didn't get to California?"

"After the war, it didn't matter to me where I went. I was disillusioned with politics and war, although I did go on to Stanford. But I missed Texas and came home eventually. All my training led to law enforcement." He paused and looked at her. "I thought that I could make a difference."

The car slowed, and Bill stopped under the yellow-leafed sycamore in front of Susanna's house.

"Here, already?" She looked at her house, light shining brightly from every window. "It looks like Clay's home too."

She reached her hand across the car seat and touched Bill's arm. "Thank you, Bill."

He took her hand. "May I see you again?" He squeezed her hand gently. "Soon?"

She felt currents rush through her body. She moved smoothly across the seat toward him, turning her face up to his, and looked into sexy, brown eyes. "Yes, I would like that very much."

He turned his body toward her, slipped an arm inside her coat and around her waist, and drew her close. She felt her breasts pressing into his chest.

He placed his left hand to her face, his fingers lightly tracing her lips, and looked into her eyes. "You are a beautiful and a brave woman, Sue Perez."

He kissed her. She responded, meeting his tongue with urgency as their hearts pounded. She broke away and slipped out of the car. Bill opened his door. She held up her hand, shaking her head, and hurried to her front porch.

"Thank you for a wonderful evening," she called softly and kissed the palm of her hand, pursing her lips to blow the kiss to him before going inside

Bill drove away.

I completely forgot about making him a cup of coffee!

CHAPTER TEN

The sky was clear and blue with full sunshine breaking the cold and spreading golden warmth on Monday morning.

"It sure enough *is* Indian summer!" Susanna said with delight as she and Leroy surveyed the work to be done at Pioneer Plants. She was clad in snug-fitting jeans and a powder blue, goose-down vest over a yellow turtleneck. Lisa had taken her mother's blue cap, so Susannah found one of Lisa's to wear—an Alpine Bucks maroon woolen cap pulled down to her brows. Her long, shiny hair extended over her shoulders.

She and Leroy walked beneath a netted section of the nursery that they had lined with plastic sheeting during the snowy week before.

"Grab hold of that end, Leroy," She pointed to a long roll of plastic on the ground. "We'll cover the sides from post to post. We should've done it already."

"Yes, ma'am," Leroy said, removing a work glove to reach for the loose end of the plastic roll. "I hafta say that the snow sure was good moisture for those seed balls and grass up on the Mill Ring."

They struggled to enclose the outdoor area by stretching and smoothing the plastic sheeting along the outer corner posts. Leroy used a staple gun to attach the plastic to the posts of the framed area.

"That oughta do it," he said and slid the staple gun into a back pocket of his canvas overalls.

Susanna removed her gloves and sat inside an open wheelbarrow, drawing her feet up and under her. "It'll be quiet here at the nursery this coming week, Leroy. I plan to do some substitute teaching again in Marfa, make some extra money before Christmas. I need to see my dad too, during the holidays." Her voice trailed off.

Leroy cleared his throat, bringing Susanna back to the present.

"Oh!" she said. "Sorry. Can you hold down the fort on the days I'm teaching?"

"Yes, ma'am. Do you know what days so I can bring my lunch?"

He looks so earnest with his brow furrowed.
"I start next Monday for a teacher on emergency leave. It might be—every day?" She watched for Leroy to nod assent. "For the next two weeks?"

* * *

Katherine caught the ringing phone in the kitchen as she poured a second cup of coffee. "Hello? This is Katherine Bell."

"Katherine?" a now-familiar voice inquired.

Good heavens, what now?

"Oh, hello, Judge Bassinger. How are you and your *wife*?" She held the phone under her chin and emptied two packets of Splenda into her coffee mug.

"Fine, fine. I wanted to tell you that the new trash collection company in town has a man doing a survey today."

"Yes, I think you called me about that." *Is this guy for real?* She poured cream in the cup and stirred. The judge was silent, and as she sipped her coffee, Katherine abruptly realized that he meant the surveyors were there *now.*

Her eyes widened, and she raised her voice. "A man is doing a survey *now*? For Dumpsters?"

"Yes. You may want to talk to him."

"They're outside my door," she mumbled with a tone of inescapability.

"Right. I asked him to meet you and find out where you'd like that new trash bin."

She rolled her eyes and set the cup on the counter. "All right," she said, expelling her breath. "I'll go out to meet him, and I'll suggest a place. Please, don't give it another thought." *Or another call.*

"Good. May I take you to dinner on Saturday evening, Ms. Bell?"

"What?" She was completely flustered. "Saturday? Oh. I thank you, *and* Mary, but no. I, I have a small dinner party planned."

Silence.

"Uhhh, would the two of you like to join us?" she spluttered.

"Why yes, I'd like that."

She could tell by his voice that he was smiling. "Yes, well." She sighed. "See you both at seven o'clock, Saturday evening, my house, casual dress."

"Thank you. I'll be there!"

Katherine hung up and puzzled over the conversation. She walked to the back door with disbelief that a surveyor could be out there. Sure enough, a stranger was parked on her side street with a clipboard and pen. He waved as she went out the iron gate to meet him.

"Where would you like your new trash bin, ma'am?"

Katherine pointed just past her driveway along her side of the street. "Over here, I guess."

"Yes, ma'am," the man agreed with a short nod.

Katherine noticed the young women from the mountainside house walking down the street toward her. They waved.

She returned a half wave and turned dismissively to her house when a voice rang out, "Wait! We want to talk to you."

Ellie and Janis trotted down the street until they stood near Katherine.

"Janis wants to know where she might take art classes. Do you know if they offer any at the university?" Ellie panted.

Katherine listened to Ellie, but her eyes turned to her sister, Janis, who painfully reminded her of her own daughter. "I wouldn't know. You might call the school and ask."

"Oh, I thought maybe you were a painter and would know," Janis said shyly.

"Not any more," Katherine answered curtly. "Sorry, I can't visit right now. I need to attend to some errands." She forced a smile and edged toward her gate.

* * *

"I may be gone for a few weeks at Christmas," Katherine said to Carmen who had arrived to clean the house. "We'll mark the calendar for those dates, so you can be off if you'd like."

Carmen stopped washing dishes and turned to watch Katherine make herself a second cup of coffee at the kitchen counter. "Where you goin'?" Carmen's speech inflection was from Mexico's Chihuahua region, bordering Texas.

"Paris," said Katherine, looking over the rim of her purple cup.

"Paris, Texas?" Carmen asked, her eyes widening.

"No." Katherine held back a smile. "There is a Paris in Texas, but I meant Paris, across the Atlantic Ocean, in Europe."

"Ohhhh, that sounds *very* nice," Carmen said grinning. "You need to go somewhere *exciting*. Maybe meet a nice man."

Katherine saw Carmen's round eyes sparkle with humor and she smiled back. "I don't think so."

She lingered, holding the warm cup in both hands, and looked up at the ceiling. Her smile faded. "I just need to be *away* somewhere for Christmas." She set the coffee cup down on the counter and mumbled under her breath, "Holidays are unbearable."

She walked through the house to her bedroom and looked at the photographs of her husband and her daughter lining the top of her bureau. The room, the house, her life, seemed hollow. She decided to busy herself with planning a party and sending invitations.

You are invited to a casual supper party this Saturday at
Katherine Bell's
804 N. Harris Street
Casual dress.   RSVP 783-2011

Katherine e-mailed the invitations to people she had met in the area if she knew their e-mail addresses. Then she printed copies to mail or hand out to acquaintances, which now included the friendly stranger Judge Harlan Bassinger *and* his wife, Mary. She looked up their street address in the phone book and thought of one more person. Turning to the J's, she found the listing for Frank and Trudy Johnson and copied the address. It might be a little soon, but it might be good for the widow to get out for an evening; at least she would know that people were thinking about her.

* * *

Trent pulled under his carport in Fort Davis as the autumn sun slipped behind the Davis Mountains. He had spent a long day on a case in Terlingua near the Texas-Mexico border, and he was tired.

He chuckled as he thought of his friend, Billy, who owned a store in the ghost town. Billy had been wooing a young lady from Alpine, and the two were attending an early Mass on a recent

Sunday morning at the Catholic Church near the border when a commotion began outside.

A trio of fleeing drug dealers had burst through the double front doors and raced straight through the church out the rectory door.

Trent had followed in hot pursuit, gun raised, boots stomping, voice yelling. As he escorted the handcuffed culprits back through the sanctuary, he had noticed Billy huddled in a corner with the terrified lady. The look in Billy's eyes was unmistakably gleeful as she clung to him. All must have gone well because Trent had heard they were to be married next week in the Alpine Catholic Church.

He opened his front door.

"Hell-o!" sang a voice from the kitchen. Trent headed straight there.

"Buenos noches, darlin'," Darlita crooned, her voice lilting. She stood smiling by the oven wearing an oven mitt on each hand and nothing else. "Supper is about ready to put on the table."

"I see you got my message that I'd be home soon."

Trent ground out his cigar stub in the kitchen sink and sniffed. "Ummmmm. You smell good."

He gathered her up like a bride and carried her down the hall. Mitts fell to the floor.

* * *

The casserole dish was still warm as Darlita placed it on a hot pad on the small kitchen table. She watched Ambrose pad barefoot back into the kitchen. He, too, was wrapped in a bathrobe. He took a glass from a cabinet, filled it with ice from the freezer, and poured two fingers of whiskey. He snatched the TV remote and clicked ON at the small television that faced the kitchen table.

Darlita sat at the table and smiled. "Come and get it."

He returned her smile. "I already have."

He lit a fresh cigar and joined her at the table. "How was your day?" he asked and pulled an ashtray toward him, balanced the cigar along its edge, and drained the whiskey. He clicked the volume up on the TV before she could answer.

"Fine," she mumbled. Then she looked from the television to him and raised her voice. "If you really want to know, turn that blasted thing down!"

He did.

"Well, not really a great day," she said with pouting lips. "The kids were a little down after losing Friday night's game."

She watched him take a bite of food and turn to her with a look of sympathy. He muted the television as a commercial began.

"And yours? Have you seen your sister, Katherine, lately?" she asked, making small talk as she picked at the plate of food. He shook his head, and she added, "She's having us to dinner on your birthday."

"Humph," he grunted. "I'd just as soon skip birthdays."

"Any news on the highway patrolman?" she asked.

"Well," he drawled and rose to refill the whiskey glass. "The composite drawings are back from Dallas on the drivers of that eighteen-wheeler, and they do know that a fourth car was at the murder scene."

He measured approximately two fingers of scotch over the remaining ice in his glass and returned to the table. "It was a small car like yours," he said casually and smiled. "Have you been going places behind my back, hon?"

She dropped her fork, and it clattered under the table. She pushed out from the table, retrieved the fork, and took her plate to the sink.

Trent studied her silently and turned back to CNN.

"I think I'll go soak in a hot tub," she said with a broad smile. "Eat your food, darlin', 'fore it gets cold." She padded down the hall.

Trent downed the whiskey and watched TV while his food grew waxy.

CHAPTER ELEVEN

It was noontime. Judge Bassinger's wife, Mary, stood at the sink of the teacher's lounge washing her hands. She wore a low-cut, print bodice with a short, black-leather skirt and spike-heeled leather boots. She turned to Susanna, who had just walked into the room.

"I saw you at the game Friday night," she said in a teasing, musical voice.

Susanna flushed and said nothing as she sat at the lunch table and unpacked her lunch from a small cooler.

"I've seen that Butler before," said Kelly. She was seated at the Formica-topped table opening a bag of carrot sticks. "He lectured once at Sam Houston State when I was a senior."

Susanna unwrapped her sandwich and looked across the table at Kelly. "Oh? Didn't Trudy and Frank Johnson go there too?"

"Yes."

Susanna took a bite of tuna salad on whole wheat bread and swallowed. "Did you know them?"

Kelly squirmed. "I was once engaged to Frank Johnson." Her lips pursed. "That is, until Trudy came along and took him away."

Susanna's forehead creased as she watched Kelly's downcast eyes, wondering if this could have any connection with the patrolman's death.

"My, my. What a small world," said Mary, pulling on her gray smock to return to the classroom.

"Right." Susanna gathered her trash. "The older I get, the more implosive my world. Those six degrees of separation are shrinking."

* * *

Doris pushed through the door of Sixth Street Bakery & Café and spotted Katherine sitting alone at a table near the back of the room.

"Sorry I'm late," Doris said and hung her purse strap over the knob of a chair.

"It's OK." Katherine shrugged with a faint smile.

Doris quickly assessed Katherine's blue mood and tried cheering her up. "Can you believe that time is going so quickly?" She sat next to Katherine at the small wooden table and added, "It's almost time for your party!"

Katherine cast her eyes down to the table.

"Hi, Ms. Bell," a voice sang.

Doris and Katherine twisted around to see two smiling women seated at a nearby table. Katherine recognized the young people from the Burkson house.

"Oh, hello," Katherine replied.

"We're getting acquainted with Alpine," an eager voice chirped. "We plan to visit the McDonald Observatory Friday night."

"Great. Dress warmly." Katherine glanced at Doris and back to the twosome. "You may remember my friend, Professor Kemp?"

The women acknowledged one another.

Katherine looked at the young woman who reminded her so much of her own daughter. "Did you find the art classes you wanted?"

"Not yet." The young woman smiled sweetly back at Katherine.

Katherine recalled Brann hovering as she held their newborn daughter. "Fathers leave an inheritance of money and property," he had said. "Mothers leave a legacy of love." He was so proud. She felt a tinge of resentment toward the vibrant young women.

"It's Stargazer Night," the sister reminded.

"You'll enjoy that," Katherine responded automatically. She pictured a summer vacation when she and Brann had visited the Davis Mountains when Maureen was about seven years old. They had sat bundled together in the open air under the stars while a guide pointed and named each star and galaxy on Stargazer Night. It had been a highlight of their family trip. They, too, were young and happy then.

She became conscious of an awkward silence and forced herself to break from the past. "It's always cold at night on the mountaintop. Be sure to dress warmly." A waxen smile creased her face as she continued, "I'm having a casual dinner party this Saturday …"

Out of the corner of her eye she saw Sam Bassinger approach.

"Hey, Miss B," he interrupted with a dazzling smile. He nodded toward the younger women. "These beautiful young ladies must be your relatives?"

Katherine didn't know whether to place him in a white or a black hat. "Sam, these are my new neighbors, and yours too. They're living on the hill just above our houses. Ellie and … " she faltered.

"Janis." The younger woman filled in her name.

"Yes." She nodded at them and back to Sam. "And this is Sam Bassinger.

"Beware," she added in a stage whisper.

"So," he grinned directly at Janis. "You're new in town? I would be happy to be your neighborly guide." He swept the cowboy hat from his head, walked closer, and bowed.

Katherine and Doris exchanged glances. Doris gave a small shrug.

"As I was saying," Katherine continued, "I'm having a dinner party at my home Saturday, at seven in the evening. I'd be pleased if you could come with your friends, Race and Frank." She lifted her eyes to Sam. "You too, Sam."

"Thank you, we will," the young women chimed.

"Count me in," Sam said grinning as he dragged an empty chair to the young women's table. He hung his hat on a chair knob and plunked himself down.

Katherine and Doris turned back to their own table as the threesome engaged in animated conversation.

"Doesn't take him long, does it," Doris whispered. "Did he shave his mustache?"

"Well yes, he did, and his goatee. I wonder what that's all about?"

"Who knows with young people nowadays." Doris threw her hands up. "These current generations mutilate themselves. And," she leaned across the table for emphasis, "most have a sense of entitlement to all they can get by any means. They look to one another for standards like castaways on an island. It seems that the older generation has no pattern they wish to follow, so they set their own. Unfortunately the lowest common denominator often rules." She backed her chair away from the table. "Shall I get more iced tea for us from the drink bar?"

"Yes, thank you," Katherine said absently while she looked around the room. Her eyes settled on Sam. He was her closest neighbor and a Bassinger. She puzzled over seeing a dark sports car in *his* driveway.

The car looked like the one that almost ran me off the road that night too. Maybe I didn't get a good enough look at the car. I sure didn't see who was driving. How many sports cars are there in this small, rural town?

Doris returned with the refills and took a seat.

"Judge Bassinger asked me out to dinner," Katherine said hesitantly when Doris looked up.

"Oh? With or without his wife?" Doris raised her eyebrows and waited for an answer.

"I'm not sure. Luckily it was for the same night as my party, not that I would have gone. But I did invite them as a couple to join us."

Doris rolled her eyes and smiled. "Well, now, I too may have a suitor, although I could be deluded."

"Let me guess. Is he at Sul Ross?" Katherine asked.

"Right. You know, a May-December kind of attraction? I've turned into the foolish older woman."

Katherine smiled. "Age doesn't seem to matter anymore."

Doris shrugged, and they ate their soup in silence.

Katherine set her spoon down. "Doris? Do you still feel married?"

There was no response.

She placed her napkin on the table beside the bowl. "Because I do."

Doris paused, her spoon in midair. "That's because you found your true love. Most of us never do."

Katherine pushed her food back and watched folks come and go in the busy café as she considered Doris's comment. "You've never said much about your late husband," she began cautiously. "Is it alright for me to ask about him?"

"He's been gone for nine years."

Doris halted, and Katherine waited for her to go on.

"All right, let me begin when things seemed perfect in my life," Doris said in a low voice. "I had a degree in law and wanted to study criminal justice—which is a subcategory of law—as well as lots of other nifty subjects, like anthropology of crime, social control, sociology of law, and so on.

"I learned, too late, in grad school for my PhD, that what the PhD is really for is to prepare teachers to churn out law enforcement and corrections officers and polish some of the latter to be administrators—hence the required study of management and statistical analyses." She pushed back her plate.

Katherine leaned over the table, completely absorbed.

"My favorite subjects turned out to be experimental design and multivariate regression theory, a fancy way to use statistical data to infer patterns," Doris continued.

"This was in graduate school?" Katherine asked.

"Yes. Other folks in my program studied criminal justice to get promotions and to validate the college teaching they were doing, or wanted to do."

"But not you?"

"No, I had the perfect job at Pan American University in the Texas Valley. I would have happily and naturally progressed to be a criminal justice researcher."

"What happened?" Katherine queried.

"At Pan Am I was with a faculty dedicated to bicultural education. I personally set up internships in Monterey, Mexico, for students the first year I was there. I taught every subject in the curriculum over a two-year period.

"I was part of the Women's Studies resource team and helped put on a women workers' conference, including *maquilador* women. I had friends and colleagues who were both Anglo and Latino. I had a community that included college and township.

"I worked with the American Friends Service Committee, a Quaker service group. I organized and directed an amnesty clinic for immigrants, training students who had vague ideas about going to law school. I was learning so many things whichever way I turned." She stopped and looked away.

"Doris! Why did you ever leave?" Katherine pushed her bowl away and sat immersed in a life that Doris hadn't revealed before now.

Doris looked pained. "It was Carl, my husband. His allergies got worse and worse. He couldn't go outdoors. He was twenty-five years older and retired from teaching when I met him."

Doris looked down.

"Please go on," Katherine urged.

"Thank you." Doris sighed. "So we had to move. When we came to Alpine, I was hired the first semester as a part-time instructor. They didn't need more than that. Later, when they offered more, Carl threatened to commit suicide if I wasn't at home—with him. I didn't know how to deal with that.

"Anything that took me away from him got that threat until I learned how to cope with the help of our doctor. By then I had turned down too many offers of employment to be credible, and Carl had become truly in need of my being with him all the time."

Her eyes were downcast and her face sad.

Katherine didn't move as she spoke to Doris. "I can't imagine those years for you ... or the nine years since he passed away."

"Of course I lost him years before he died," Doris replied, smoothing the napkin in her lap. "He had Alzheimer's."

Katherine face effected horror. "I'm so sorry."

"There are worse things than death, Katherine," Doris stated, looking down while wringing the napkin in her lap.

"Nine years is a long time to be alone," Katherine sympathized.

"Well, I did go back to work at the university. And I know now that there are *also* worse things than being alone." Doris paused and looked up at Katherine with a grin. "Even though a companion would be welcome, at this stage of my life there's a place inside of me where I'm never alone."

"What does that mean?"

"It means that I believe in a participating deity."

Katherine looked puzzled. "I don't understand."

"It means for me, there is a God who is there, offering fellowship and safety and a pathway in this wilderness."

"How do you know 'God' is there?" Katherine asked.

"A presence. I sought and found this presence, and I live in that presence and it lives in me."

"That's what's said of the universe," Katherine said thoughtfully. "We live in the universe, and being made of the same stuff as the stars, the universe lives in us."

"Well, maybe the *universe*," Doris curled two fingers to form quotation marks, "is another word for God. After all, mankind made up words to identify and communicate."

Katherine slowly nodded. They sat in silence for several moments.

"Doris, I must tell you that the least friendly people in Far West Texas have been the church people. Not one, in the time I've been here, has invited me to their service. And the few times I've attended one or another, only one couple from Fort Davis has invited me to their home. It's hard to reconcile the presence of God with these clannish people who ignore a stranger in their midst."

Doris groaned. "I know. Many mistake church for a club with selective membership, skeptical of any newcomer. That presence I spoke about? It's rare to find in a church building these days."

Katherine made no response. She placed her napkin on the table and opened her patterned cloth wallet. "I'll get this." She pulled out a twenty-dollar bill.

"Oh, I almost forgot," she said. "When Susanna called, she told me that her principal used to be engaged to *Frank Johnson* at Sam Houston State, before he met Trudy."

"That's interesting," Doris responded. "Maybe she never got over him?"

"And killed him?" Katherine stifled a chuckle.

Doris lowered her eyes, obviously lost in thought.

"So? Should we tell my brother or Captain Butler?" Katherine asked.

"Well, yes." Doris pulled some loose dollar bills from her purse for a tip. "My turn to get lunch next week." She weighted the bills with a saltshaker in the center of the table.

CHAPTER TWELVE

"It seems that the guys in that particular eighteen-wheeler came through here often." Sheriff Carlton spoke to Ranger Trent and Captain Butler past the boots he'd propped on his desk.

He shoved a printout across the desk. "Their names are Scrim Clark and Lito Vasquez. They both served hard time. Different prisons. But they've been clean since and report to their parole officers like clockwork."

Butler looked at the photos over Trent's shoulder. "Mutt and Jeff. Clark's the big guy, I take it?"

"Yeah. A pretty boy," said the sheriff.

Trent tapped the pages. "So where are they now?"

"We don't know," Carlton answered. "A visit's due with each of their parole officers. I've put out an APB to pull them in for questioning."

Butler squinted at the papers Trent handed him. "Bassinger and Compton still insist on not knowing where the truck went?"

"Yep," Carlton said. "Got paid in hard cash they say and told to ask no questions. Bassinger says he met Scrim in a local bar while playing pool this summer. Says he saw him a few times after that, same bar, and set up this onetime deal."

"What bar?" Butler asked.

"Zeppie's on Holland Avenue," Trent interjected. "We've questioned Zeppie and his bar staff several times. I know most of them. Darlita and I meet friends there often on weekends when I'm off work."

"Many of the locals are regulars at Zeppie's," Carlton said, yanking his boots down from the desktop and standing up. He adjusted the gun on his hip. "They serve a good steak, get a good crowd. Which makes me hungry! Y'all interested in going there for lunch?"

* * *

Sam Bassinger drove his truck out of Marathon toward Alpine. As he neared his adobe house next to Katherine Bell's, he glanced up at the rearview mirror and saw flashing red lights.

"What now?" he moaned and jerked his pickup to the right side of the street. "They've come to get me," he told Rasputin who lay on the seat beside him.

He stopped the truck abruptly, pressed buttons to open the windows, cut the engine, and slid to the passenger side of the cab. He lifted Rasputin and pushed him behind the steering wheel, placing his big puppy paws on the wheel.

"We might as well have a little fun!"

Sam leaned back against the passenger seat and waited. A police officer cautiously approached and looked through the window.

Sam leaned an earnest face toward the open window and said, "Thank *God* you stopped him, officer! He would have killed us *all*!"

The policeman stepped back and half grinned. "Sam, get your taillight fixed!" He put his pen and book of tickets down to his side and walked back to his vehicle shaking his head.

Sam watched the cop car start up, signal a left turn, and pull back onto the street.

Back in place as the driver, Sam pulled onto the street and made a right turn into his driveway. A BMW M3 black coupe sat in front of his ancient adobe walls.

He stomped on the brake. "What's *she* doing here again!"

* * *

Carmen helped Javier pour white sand into crisp brown paper lunch sacks and steady a short candle inside each.

"I'll light the luminarias at dark," Javier said as he and Carmen staged hundreds of brown bags at regular intervals along the top of the six-foot adobe walls surrounding Katherine's front yard.

"*Muy bonita!*" Carmen exclaimed, clapping her hands as she surveyed their work.

She looked up as a Gage Hotel delivery truck from Marathon pulled into the driveway, and watched men begin to unload boxes at Katherine's back door.

"I'd better go help Ms. Bell with the food," she said to Javier.

She went inside the house looking for her employer. Katherine was setting out silver and china and arranging bottles of wine and glasses in the kitchen.

Her head lifted at Carmen's approach, and she smiled. "We're set. Thank you for helping. Will you be able to stay?"

"Javier and I will stay as long as you need us. He has to light the luminarias. There are so *meeny!*"

"Wonderful!" Katherine smiled and enlisted Carmen's help with getting white wines and soft drinks into iced coolers.

A Gage Hotel deliveryman returned with an invoice for Katherine to sign.

* * *

"But, Mom," whined Clay, "I don't want you to go out with him!"

"Why not?"

"He's not my dad!"

Susanna breathed a loud sigh. "Clay, no one will ever take your dad's place. No one. Captain Butler is just trying to be nice to you. And to me."

Lisa crept inside Clay's bedroom where the discussion was taking place. "It's embarrassing, Mom! My friends are asking questions." Her voice was as dramatic as her stomping exit.

Susanna continued to place folded clothes in a chest of drawers in Clay's bedroom. She hadn't thought that dating again would cause such trauma for her children. Maybe she should just cancel going with Bill to Katherine's party tonight.

She reached for the phone, thinking that this kind of anguish wasn't worth it. She left a message telling Bill not to pick her up, that she would meet him at Katherine's house.

* * *

"Hi, Steven." Katherine smiled happily, opening her back door and holding it for three men carrying worn black cases for guitars, a fiddle, and a banjo. "I see you're here early with your gear. Welcome."

Katherine thought back on how many years she had known Steven and his talented artist wife, Allie—back to college years at Texas Christian University in Fort Worth.

"Where should we put these?" Steven asked.

"How about in this back room," Katherine said, guiding them into her office space, a converted second bedroom. "It's *so nice* that you're providing entertainment for my party! Thank you! Put your gear and jackets anywhere in here."

"That's what friends are for." Steven grinned.

"I appreciate it, beyond the telling." She met his eyes with gratitude.

Pete grinned and announced, "We've decided to call ourselves the Desert-Mountain Boys."

"You certainly have a large enough group of *stars* that've come to this area," she replied, remembering that Steven and Tad had played with several Texas groups in the past, including Asleep at the Wheel and the Austin Lounge Lizards. And Pete—he knew enough about music and musicians to write books.

"How's your shop doing?"

"It's doing well," Pete answered. "Oh, by the way. Mary and the other gals will be along a little later. You know how much time it takes you wimmen to get ready." His grin was wide. "We wanted to get here, set up, tune up, and wait for the others who are comin' to play with us."

"Can I get you something to drink?" Katherine asked.

All three nodded. "Sure."

The phone rang.

"Do you mind helping yourselves while I get that? Cold beer, wine, water, and soft drinks are in the kitchen."

Katherine rushed to her bedroom, chuckling at the thought of it being Judge Bassinger on the phone.

"Hello. This is Katherine Bell."

"Katherine! Doris. May I bring a guest to your party?"

Katherine was amused to hear the excitement in Doris's voice.

"Of course! Anyone you want to bring is welcome. Come on over. Susanna is coming with Bill Butler."

"Oh, good. See you soon." Click.

The front doorbell rang, and Katherine made her way there, opening the door wide to greet her brother and his wife.

"We're not too early, are we?" Darlita asked, looking around at the empty room, her black eyes and hair sparkling.

"No, no. You're right on time," Katherine said. "You look dazzling, Darlita." She embraced her sister-in-law. "Come in."

Ambrose removed his white hat and handed her a bottle of Souza, Tequila Gold. "For you, Sis," he said with a slight bow.

Before Katherine could utter a word of thanks, Kelly Krimshaw hollered from inside the front gate, "Hey, Katherine! The *candelarias* along your walls are beautiful!"

Kelly had barely closed the solid wooden gate when it popped open again, and Katherine's new neighbors from the house on Hancock Hill crowded through.

"We've never seen lights like this in Chicago," Ellie gushed. "How festive! Are they traditional?"

"Yes. They're luminarias. I got the idea in Santa Fe, New Mexico," Katherine said. "Everybody come on in." She showed the ladies to her bedroom where they placed their purses and jackets across the bed.

Bananas greeted people, wagging her tail and going from person to person.

The back doorbell rang. Katherine went to get it and saw Doris at the door dressed up more than usual and wearing makeup. A slender and attractive man stood next to her. Katherine pushed the screen door open and greeted them.

Doris smiled. "Katherine, this is Sandy Wisner." She looked back at Sandy. "And this is my friend, Katherine Bell."

Sandy stood stiffly. "It is a distinct honor, Mrs. Bell."

He's sure nervous, Katherine thought and reached her hand out to shake his. "Come in, come in."

A fire glowed in the living room, and Javier poured drinks for guests while Carmen carried the last-minute food items to the dining room table.

Katherine went to the front door and pushed it open, thinking that arriving guests should feel free to walk in. She had just propped it back when she heard the gate creak open and a voice ring out.

"Good evening, Ms. Bell."

Katherine looked up to see the latest arrivals.

"Oh, hello, Judge Bassinger." She walked out on the small front porch. "I'm glad you two could make it."

She was surprised at how distinguished he was, tall and handsome with hair graying at the temples.

And his wife ... *if she wasn't an aging Dolly Parton!*

Mary's long, red hair was poofed up high with large curls falling around her small shoulders. Katherine quickly reviewed her attire: a snug, lace-up jacket over a low-cut ruffled blouse that exposed freckled, bubbling cleavage. The skirt was tight and hit above her knees, showing off shapely little legs teetering on three-inch high heels, the glitter of a diamond bracelet on one ankle.

They climbed the front steps to meet Katherine on the porch. "Please, call me Harlan," the judge said, handing her a bouquet of colorful, fresh-cut flowers: anemones, Michelmas daisies, asters, and goldenrod.

"These are for our lovely hostess."

Katherine took the large bouquet in her arms. "How thoughtful. Thank you, Harlan; thank you, Mary. Won't you come in? I was just leaving the door open so that people could just walk in as they arrive."

"Yes, my pleasure," he drawled.

Katherine could finally connect that deep, rich baritone voice with the phone calls. He stepped into the house with Mary close behind.

Katherine felt happy as she looked across the rooms and saw people gathered in small groups, holding drinks and plates of food, and busily talking to one another. Bananas was making the rounds.

"Excuse me, Mary, Harlan; I see some friends coming in the back."

Susanna had walked through the back door. Katherine thought that she had never seen Susanna sparkle like she did tonight, but her eyes looked sad.

Katherine met her and gave her a hug. "Where's Bill?"

"It's a long story," Susanna answered. "Tell you later."

A musician came up behind Katherine with guitar in hand and tapped her on the shoulder. She turned toward him smiling.

"Would you like us to play now?" he asked.

"Yes, thank you."

"Will do."

Katherine watched him cross the room to his buddies and noticed that several more musicians had arrived to add their gifts to the music offering. As she turned back to Susanna, she caught a flash of someone crossing the back of her yard. *Oh well,* she thought, *they can see the porch lights to find the door.*

She heard strains of "I've Got Spurs That Jingle Jangle Jingle" coming from the living room. She crossed to the big open room and watched her new neighbors gather around the musicians with looks of awe.

"Katherine," someone whispered urgently in her ear. She pulled back and scrutinized Sam Bassinger, who was scowling. *Is he up to something?*

He motioned for her to follow him out to the back porch, which she did reluctantly.

"What is it, Sam?"

He pointed to the silhouette of a woman standing in the shadows of the backyard. "It's Trudy Johnson! She was out there when I came in."

Katherine strained her eyes to see, but the small figure retreated into darkness. She felt alarm.

"What's going on, Sam?"

"I don't know. I went out and asked her to come in, but she said no, she didn't think she should. She asked to speak to my dad."

Sam looked as upset as Katherine felt.

"I invited Trudy to the party," Katherine said. "But what is she doing out there?"

"I'm afraid she won't go away until she speaks to my dad," Sam said tersely.

"Then I think you should go tell *him* what you just told me. I'll see if I can get her to come up to the porch."

Sam nodded and hastened inside. Katherine edged to the steps of the porch and called out to the darkness, "Trudy? This is Katherine. Won't you come to the porch?"

No answer.

"Trudy? Are you still there? Sam went to get Judge Bassinger for you."

"Yes," called a small voice. "Just send him out here, please. I hafta talk to him."

"Alright," Katherine called back. "You can wait on the porch if you'd like."

This is too strange for words. Has she lost her mind? Was Harlan a family friend? Was Trudy's little boy with her parents? Did they know she was out tonight?

Her heart lurched when the screen door slammed. She looked back to see Harlan come out, his forehead creased deeply and his face deathly pale.

"Where is she?" he asked curtly.

"Out here, Harlan," Trudy cried. "I need to talk to ya, fer jest a minute."

Katherine watched the judge start out to the yard. "Do you need any help?" she called to him softly.

He turned back, putting his finger to his lips and shaking his head. "No, no. Everything will be all right. I'm sure she's distraught over her husband's death. I'll see that she gets home. Will you let my wife know? So sorry, Ms. Bell."

Thinking that her presence might further upset Trudy, Katherine slipped back inside, deeply concerned for the young widow.

Music from an acoustic guitar, a bass, fiddle, and her upright piano filled the front room. For a moment, she thought she heard Trudy's sobs blowing in the late October wind, or maybe it was her imagination.

Katherine looked across the room at the musicians, their wives, and her new neighbors. Race was putting more wood on the fire, Janis and Ellie were seated with their drinks and food, and she felt comforted. And, *would you look at that*! Bill Butler had arrived and was seated close to Susanna on a sofa, his hand on hers.

Katherine didn't want to break the spell of the evening, so she slipped back to her bathroom to compose herself. A moment later she heard a determined rap, rap, rap at the bathroom door and opened it.

"Are you all right?" Doris queried, worry written all over her face. "I saw you come in from the back just now."

Katherine pulled Doris inside the bathroom, shut the door, and told her of the episode with Trudy.

"Maybe we could go over tomorrow or Monday and assure her that she can't possibly experience all of her grief at once—that one can't survive that much shock," Doris suggested.

Katherine looked down to consider the ever-creeping reality of death. She gulped and looked up at Doris.

"Meanwhile," happiness shone in Doris's eyes, "I want you to tell me what you think of Sandy." She affected a worried look. "Do I look like his mother?"

This snapped Katherine back to the present. "Of course not!" she assured. She took a deep breath and added, "I'll pay more attention to him. Let's rejoin the party."

Doris returned to Sandy, and Katherine went for a glass of wine, trying to shake her troubled feelings. Near the kitchen, she passed behind Sam and overheard his conversation with Janis.

"Well, if you want an active social life out here, you need to join the Catholic Church or Alcoholics Anonymous."

Janis's laugh sounded uneasy to Katherine. She stole a look at Janis around Sam and shook her head, mouthing, "Don't pay any attention to him."

Katherine approached the bar set up in the kitchen. "Javier, thank you for staying. May I have a glass of red wine? And please, you and Carmen feel free to join the party at any time."

"Thank you, Miss Katherine," he said, "but I need to get home to my family. I'll tell Carmen."

Katherine took the glass of wine and carried it into the dining room where she served herself food on a small plate. She continued around the dining table to stand near Sandy Wisner, who was having an animated conversation with Ellie.

"Were you here this spring?" Katherine heard Sandy ask.

Ellie shook her head, and Sandy continued, "When you see the buzzards circling Hancock Hill, you know that spring has arrived in Alpine."

Ellie nodded. "A lady downtown was telling me about this. She told about the time that she saw the buzzards flying in formation north from Mexico—and a brown pelican was right there, in formation with them!"

They laughed together.

"It's true," Sandy said, and began another anecdote on Alpine phenomena.

Katherine excused herself and took her plate into the TV room and sat near Doris and the group assembled there. She nodded to Frank and Race, who were seated between Kelly Krimshaw and Doris.

"I just heard Sandy telling about the buzzards circling Hancock Hill," Katherine said to Kelly.

Kelly leaned toward Katherine and whispered, "Did you know that Sandy Wisner is Judge Bassinger's nephew?"

"No." Katherine shook her head and glanced at Doris, who was in quiet conversation with Race.

"Yes, his *mother* was a Bassinger before she married Keith Wisner."

Katherine realized that Kelly relished this story and felt dread in hearing the rest of it.

"Keith had a heart attack when he was only forty-five, and then Sandy's mother, whom Sandy *adored,* died of a staph infection after surgery a few years ago. Judge Bassinger has been supporting and putting him through school at Sul Ross, even though Sandy's certainly old enough to be on his own."

This town is beginning to sound incestuous, thought Katherine. *I'm not sure I like getting acquainted.*

"Some people are late bloomers," she defended and turned to her other guests.

Voices from the front room broke forth loudly in a chorus from an old cowboy song. Katherine went into the other room to listen. She noticed that the age-old cowboy songs, so different from the music she had known, made her feel good. Of course, her third glass of wine might be harmonizing.

Several people came up to thank her and say good night. Katherine thought she saw tears in Susanna's eyes when she left in a hurry out the back door. Butler, obviously angry, left in a huff out the front. She stooped down to pet Bananas at her feet and quizzed, "What's going on with those two?"

After bidding most of the crowd good night, Katherine sat back in a rocking chair near the fireplace with the few guests remaining. Bananas jumped into her lap.

Sandy Wisner was telling Doris a story of a motorcycle trip to Mexico with his first cousin, Sam Bassinger. "We found a little hole-in-the-wall restaurant after a day of drinking that blue agave juice." He winked at Katherine.

Katherine realized that Sandy was currently emboldened by a good amount of "juice."

"We ordered what we considered safe. *Cabrito!*" He translated an aside to Ellie sitting nearby. "Goat."

He laughed when she wrinkled her nose and continued his tale. "When our order—of dubious pedigree—arrived, Sam and I sat silently staring at it. Finally, Sam with a straight face said gravely, 'I'd give a hundred dollars to hear a dog bark.'"

Sandy slapped his knee in mirth, and the others joined in. After the laughter died and idle chatter began anew in the room, Katherine caught Sandy's eye. "Maybe you can find out from your uncle how Trudy Johnson is doing? And let me know?"

The question visibly upset him. Sandy darted his eyes furtively around the room and walked away without saying a word.

Katherine leaned down and whispered in Bananas's ear, "Good heavens. If this weren't a small town, I'd think there was a conspiracy in the Bassinger family."

CHAPTER THIRTEEN

"I found the Criminal Justice Department here very backward; they actually gave upper-division students true-false tests while supposedly preparing them for a profession requiring daily writing of reports," Doris explained as she and Sandy sat in a downtown coffee shop where they had agreed to meet the morning after Katherine's party.

"It was as if they didn't want their students to learn how to evaluate professional research or literature. I was told specifically that it wasn't necessary."

Sandy's jaw dropped at this revelation, and she hastened to add, "They have newer staff now who are much better, and decidedly not so right wing, politically. I, for one, am trying to prepare these students for the real world."

"Hip, hip, hoorah." Sandy saluted with a straight face. Doris smiled at his theatrical flair.

"As for me," he said, "no more criminal studies. I'm done here in one year and have decided that botany is my calling. My fervent hope is to get involved experientially in pollen transfer via bees."

Doris couldn't help but giggle. "Are you serious?"

She saw his propped elbow slip from the table, and he raised the fallen hand to rub his temple.

"Are you all right?" she asked, reaching across the table for his hand.

"My kind lady, I am in dire need of the hair of the dog that bit me last evening."

His smile looked wan to Doris and his face pallid. "May I fix you something at my house?" she offered quickly.

Even as she spoke she recognized the pattern. She was infatuated. She had never experienced what Katherine had—being in love; her relationships tended toward autonomy and codependent interaction.

To hell with psychobabble. Here's a beautiful man sitting right across the table from me.

"That would be delightful!" Sandy said as he rose from the table and eased his hand over hers.

* * *

"Mom! Telephone," Lisa called to Susanna who was still lounging in bed watching the ten o'clock news that Sunday morning.

"Mom! Telephone!" Lisa called again from the kitchen and tipped a Diet Dr Pepper to her lips.

After no response, Lisa tramped down the hallway in her pajamas and bunny slippers and into her mother's bedroom.

"Mom! It's a phone call about Papaw!"

Susanna opened her eyes and reached for the telephone beside her bed. "This is Susanna Perez."

She listened and threw a glance at her daughter standing in the doorway.

"When?" She threw back the covers and sat up in bed.

"Where is he?"

She reached for a pencil and pad.

"Intensive care?"

Susanna watched Clay run into the room, still in his pajamas, squinting through sleepy eyes. "Is Papaw calling?" he asked.

"Sssshhh," his sister reproved.

Susanna began writing numbers. "Yes. My children and I will be there as soon as possible. It will take six hours whether we drive or fly. Yes. Thank you."

She hung up and motioned her kids to join her on the bed. They scampered to her, and Susanna spread her arms and hugged them to herself.

"Papaw," she began haltingly, "has been taken to a hospital in Amarillo."

She looked at Clay's wide eyes and the fear mirrored in Lisa's.

Best they know the truth.

"Papaw is very old—and weak. We may not get there before ... before he's gone."

Clay burst into tears, and Susanna held him closer. "But we'll try to make it to tell him good-bye." She hugged them tight as tears coursed her own face.

"Now," she said in her most efficient schoolmarm voice, "go pack a few everyday clothes and one Sunday outfit each. Don't forget socks and underwear."

"Mom, can't we fly out of Midland? Wouldn't that be quicker?" Lisa asked.

"The drive from here to Midland is almost three hours, plus a three-hour flight that has to stop in Dallas before going to Amarillo, Lisa. Then we'd need to rent a car," Susanna explained calmly. "Do you understand that driving our own truck is quicker? Now scat! We'll leave in less than an hour."

The kids rushed out. Susanna picked up the telephone and dialed Katherine, who answered on the second ring. Susanna explained what had happened to her dad and asked if Katherine would call Leroy Jones and tell him what happened. "And tell him that I'll call him at the nursery when I know the state of things," Susanna added.

"And Katherine? Please let Doris and Bill Butler know. There isn't time for me to talk to everyone because the kids and I need to get on the road as soon as possible."

Susanna carried the phone with her as she pulled items from her closet and chest of drawers to pack.

"Yes, I will," Katherine said. "Anything else?"

"I'm sorry to saddle you with all these calls, but I would so appreciate it if you would also call my principal, Kelly Krimshaw, so she can find a substitute for my classroom. Just a minute; I'll give you her number in Marfa."

She located her address book in the drawer of the bedside table, found the number, and read it. She also gave Katherine her own cell phone number and the number at her dad's ranch house.

"Got it," Katherine said. "I'll take care of this immediately. Don't worry about anything here. Do you need me to bring in your mail or do anything at your house?"

"I don't think so, Katherine. I'll call you if that changes. Thank you so much." She scurried about to finish packing.

I hope we get there in time!

* * *

Doris sat pondering her relationship with Sandy, if you could call it that. She was mystified; Sandy had changed his mind about coming over and had abruptly left her in the parking lot of the coffee shop with feeble excuses.

The phone rang. It was Katherine calling with the news that Susanna's dad was critically ill. Doris knew a trip to the Texas Panhandle wasn't possible for her at this time. Too much was at stake in her quest for promotion. Katherine asked her to lunch tomorrow to plan ways to help Susanna.

CHAPTER FOURTEEN

"Good morning, Carmen." Katherine greeted the housekeeper as she came through the back door the following morning.

"Did you get rested over the weekend?"

"Yes, ma'am." Carmen smiled broadly at Katherine. "Is there anything special you need done today?" She pulled her arms from a Sul Ross Lobos cotton jersey jacket and placed it with her small plastic purse and car keys near the back door. "I need to leave a little early to go to Mr. Sam's house today."

"Bassinger?" Katherine queried.

"Uh huh."

"I didn't realize that you worked at the Bassinger house." Katherine sat in her leather chair in front of the television news holding her favorite coffee cup. She clicked Mute on the remote control.

"I work for his father too," Carmen said.

"Are they nice to work for?"

"Oh my goodness, they run strange places." Carmen tsk-tsked and shook her head. "That nephew has been over digging in the judge's yard. In October, mind you."

Carmen turned around quickly at the sound of Bananas scratching at the door. She turned and talked baby talk. "Oh, Mama, you wanna come in?" She opened the door for the little dog to scamper inside, tail swishing.

Katherine knew that Bananas was excited, not only because Carmen was affectionate, but she also brought treats.

"So, you work every weekday, Carmen?" Katherine placed her hot cup on a coaster on her side table.

"Yes, ma'am. And when you need me, like this past Saturday."

"Yes, thank you, Carmen. I do appreciate your coming for the party. How many extra hours do I owe you?"

"Five," Carmen answered as she crossed the room. "Three mornings I work for you, and two for the Bassingers." She stopped in the doorway. "He's got company or something going on, and he asked me to come early and leave early ... if you don't mind me leaving an hour sooner today?"

"Of course not. Go right ahead," Katherine assured.

"Thank you," Carmen said and went toward the kitchen.

Katherine clicked the TV sound on again, waiting to see if there were wars someplace new today. Almost as quickly, she turned it off, thinking of Susanna and puzzling over her strange neighbor, Sam, and all the Bassingers.

* * *

"Sheriff," the ranger said on his cell phone, "Trent here." He looked out his car window. "The bartender from Zeppie's says he can identify those truck drivers. He'll be at your office about eleven this morning with a formal statement."

"Say, I have good news," Sheriff Carlton countered. "Just in. Those drivers, Clark and Vasquez, have been picked up in Pecos. They're being held in the county jail."

Trent heard satisfaction in the sheriff's voice.

"Are you bringin' 'em here, or goin' over there?" Trent asked as he pulled his vehicle to the side of Highway 118 outside of Fort Davis and stopped.

He knew there were dead spots for a cellular phone in the winding mountains passes ahead. Best to get the message loud and clear and have a smoke. He pulled a cigar from his pocket and opened the car window.

"It's your call," Carlton said. "We could have the bartender wait and come to my office later. That is, if we bring Clark and Vasquez here."

"Right," Trent said out of the corner of his mouth while holding a flame to the cigar. He puckered hard to get the thing going and blew a fragrant cloud out the window.

"Let's do that." He spit a small piece of tobacco from his tongue. "Let Buddy know it's OK with me. He's the bartender."

"Will do. We also have a list of foreign-made car owners in the vicinity, those registered with the county tax offices. Wanna see it?"

"Yeah, I'll be there in less than an hour. You might give Butler a call to come."

"Sure thing. See you soon."

Trent carefully laid his cigar in the ashtray and sat still. *Sure, Darlita has a little sports car, but she couldn't be involved in anything criminal.* He glanced out at the beauty of the Desert Mountains around him.

I wonder where she spends those evenings when I'm away? Oh hell, being a lawman makes anybody paranoid.

He reached for his phone and called his wife. He knew Darlita turned off her cell phone while she tutored students, but he needed to leave her a message.

Damn! I have to know where she was on the night of Johnson's murder—just to clear the air.

* * *

Mary Bassinger took longer than usual applying makeup and fixing her hair for school. She gazed intently into her bathroom mirror, scrutinizing her face and body from every angle.

"Thank God I didn't lose in the gene pool like that frumpy Doris Kemp!" she told the looking glass.

Looks had always been her meal ticket. Now past retirement age, she knew her years were beginning to show, in spite of a trim figure and an expensive facelift. Regular Botox injections smoothed wrinkles from her forehead and held off the aging process—to her face. The rest of her body was another story she thought, as she closely examined a crinkled chest, sagging upper arms, and spider veins in her legs.

"Gravity wins," she groaned.

She thought about how she had met Harlan when she was forty years old, separated from her second husband. She'd never had or wanted children. She'd gone back to school, Sul Ross State University in Alpine, to get a degree and a teaching certificate when she first met the tall, handsome lawyer, five years her junior and married with a school-age son at the time.

Mary had seen life's promise foreclose on her widowed mother at age sixty, and she didn't plan to repeat that pattern. It didn't take her long to get what she wanted; Harlan had a roving eye.

She graduated and landed a job teaching high school in nearby Marfa. The lawyer got a divorce, and the estranged Mrs. Bassinger moved to Midland with their son, Sam.

Mary and Harlan wed six weeks later. She continued teaching school, even when Harlan became a district judge. She liked getting dressed up every day and having others to talk to since she and the judge had little to talk about.

She slipped on lacy black panties and the matching bra, and admired her reflection. At least the fellas at Zeppie's still noticed. Lately she and Kelly Krimshaw had been going there for drinks in the evenings when Harlan met with lawyers to do whatever they do. He was often preoccupied for days, and going out helped her fill the lonely evenings. And besides, she liked knowing she could still attract admirers.

There was a knock at the bathroom door.

"Mary," Harlan called.

"I'm gettin' ready for school."

"I want to talk to you a minute."

She opened the door clad in panties and bra. He looked down at his little wife and pulled her to him. "Darling, you can sure ring my bell."

"Well, being too tired most nights for cuddlin' is no way to ring mine!" She pushed away.

Her eyes widened, and his softened.

"You know I have work to do," he defended.

"Harlan, you have a wandering eye, and don't think I don't know it!"

"You let Kelly use my car to meet that worthless son of mine while you sat and drank with strangers 'til all hours!" he sputtered. His face was flushed, and his temples visibly pounded. "That's no way for a judge's wife to behave!"

* * *

Butler sat at his desk thinking about Susanna. He recalled the years that he'd lectured himself in the mirror, "You will never marry again!" And now this slip of a girl had hogtied his thoughts and feelings in no time flat.

It's no good. My work is all consuming.

He thought of his former marriage broken by long and steady absences. His ex-wife still called, talking mostly about their daughter. And ex though she was, she had proved skillful at throwing subtle monkey wrenches into more than one of his relationships over the years.

"A call for you, Captain. Line one—a Ms. Perez."

Bill pushed the button for line one. "Hey, girl."

"Hi, Bill."

He heard a catch in her voice.

"I'm in the Panhandle, and I have sad news. My dad died last night."

He could hear the tightness in her voice, barely in control.

"I'm sorry, Susanna. I'd do anything to make things easier for you."

Silence.

"Do you want me to come up there?"

"Thank you, Bill. No. It's too far for you to come. And I think it would be awkward for my kids."

She paused. "The funeral will be on Wednesday." Her voice gained composure. "The kids and I should be back in Alpine by Thursday night ... if I can finish all this paperwork."

"Did you get there before ..." Bill ventured.

"I did. Dad and I said our good-byes. That means a lot to me—and the kids."

"Where's the funeral?"

"At my dad's ranch. He wanted to be buried in a pine box behind the house in my mother's garden. She's there too."

Silence.

"How's Clay and your daughter?" Bill spun the chair away from his desk and looked out the back office window. Pronghorn antelope grazed in an expanse of grassland behind his building. The foothills of the Davis Mountains rolled upward, blue in the distance.

"It's hard, of course. They have no father or living grandparents now."

Her voice sounded so small.

"I can contact anyone you like," Bill said. "Do you want Katherine and Doris to know? Do you want them to come?" He pulled a fresh sheet of notepaper from a desk drawer to make a list.

"Oh, I don't think they'd be able to do that." Her voice trailed off.

Silence.

Butler could imagine Susanna, strong and graceful, grappling with emotions, biting her lower lip. Then he heard her voice strengthen with typical Texas grit.

"Thank you so much, Bill. It helps. just to talk to you. I'll make those calls right now. May I call you again?"

He seized a pen. "Absolutely! Give me the time of the funeral and directions, just in case."

He jotted the information on the paper.

* * *

Doris drove her yellow Volkswagen faster so she would be on time for lunch with Katherine. She had loads of papers to grade, and they were piled high in her passenger seat. She wound the handle to open her window and grab some fresh air.

"Aahh, late October!"

A gust of wind scattered the papers in all directions. She snatched this way and that while she struggled to close the window. By the time she reached Sixth Street, she was a mess—hot, agitated, and late. She circled the block twice looking for a parking space.

Why was today so busy?

Finally a pickup vacated a spot right in front of the café; unfortunately she was headed in the opposite direction.

"Why me?" she wailed.

She slammed on her brake to keep from hitting a car moving out from the curb in front of her. It left an open parking place, and she slipped her small car into it. She grabbed her handsome new walking cane and pushed it out the door first in her rush across the street, her silk, tan-and-black-checkered scarf and long wool coat flapping behind her.

She saw Katherine's slender figure standing just inside the entrance looking at glass cases filled with pastries.

"I thought I was late!" Doris said, rolling her eyes as she joined her friend.

"Oh no, I just got here a moment ago. Look at those goodies!" Katherine said and giggled. She pointed at lemon bars and a tray of large oatmeal cookies sitting next to fresh cinnamon rolls, hot icing oozing.

"It's a conspiracy!" Doris quipped.

"Let's order dessert for lunch!" Katherine blurted.

Doris pushed her fists down at each side. "If I gain another pound I swear I'll run howling through the canyons! But," she chuckled, "let's do it."

They placed their orders at the counter.

"It's too chilly to sit outside by the sidewalk. How about here?" Katherine gestured toward a small table next to the window.

Doris closed her eyes with resignation, nodded, and removed her new black coat to reveal a creamy beige pantsuit. Pearls hung around her neck and from her earlobes.

Surprise surfaced on Katherine's face. "Doris! You look stunning today!"

"Thank you," Doris said in a business manner. "We spoke of a plan for advancement? Remember?"

"I do remember. My, you are a quick study," Katherine said.

They wiggled into their seats and reviewed the menu.

After ordering, Katherine's tone was somber. "What can we do that will help Susanna the most?"

"I've arranged with a church group to have casseroles delivered every day for a week when she returns," Doris responded. "And several professors at Sul Ross have signed up to take salads or casseroles by—the kind kids like."

Katherine eyed the pastry counter near the front door. "I can drop a dessert by each day."

Their food arrived, and they ate in silence.

When the plates were cleared from their table, Doris said, "Death, like taxes, is inevitable." She made eye contact with Katherine and added, "But finding this killer is important to me. It would not only be a service to the community, but it would validate my studies and teaching, especially to the university. Do you think me coldhearted?"

Katherine smiled reassuringly. "No. I know you to be curious, compassionate, and ambitious. There is nothing wrong with any of those traits. And I'm thankful to be able to help you so I can get away from my own problems."

She took a pen and notepad from her purse. "Shall we list the suspects?" She wrote the word "Suspects," underlined it, and looked up at Doris expectantly.

"You are very kind," Doris acknowledged. She smiled broadly and added, "And very organized today. OK. One: drug dealers. Frank may have routinely stopped the truck and found contraband."

"Right," Katherine said and listed "Drug dealers."

"Two: illegal aliens. They are desperate people."

Katherine nodded and wrote "Illegals."

"Three: Kelly Krimshaw. She was in love with Frank Johnson, and he jilted her."

Katherine hesitated but put "Kelly" on the list. She tapped her pen.

"There may have been another woman in his life," Doris said. "Someone we don't know about."

"Frank?" Katherine's eyes widened with disbelief. "With a beautiful wife like Trudy and a little boy he adored? No way!"

"Nevertheless," Doris said and pointed to the list.

Katherine reluctantly wrote "Lover" on the list. "That's five, and we should add 'Unknown' of course."

Doris looked up to see Sam Bassinger and one of the young women from Chicago walk to a table on the other side of the dining area.

"Look who's wasting no time," Doris whispered as she leaned toward Katherine. "That's a ladies' man for sure."

Katherine caught Janis's smile and waved back across the room.

Doris felt a tap on her shoulder and looked up to see Sandy Wisner standing next to her with a fixed smile.

"Sandy!" she exclaimed. *I cannot figure out this man!* "How are you feeling? Won't you join us?"

Sandy assented and looked at Katherine, who smiled a welcome. He shifted around Doris to pull a chair from the table.

"Remember Sandy?" Doris looked at Katherine and back at Sandy. "He came with me to your party?"

"Yes, of course I remember." Katherine smiled. "Hello, Sandy."

He gave a curt nod of recognition and pulled his chair closer to the table.

"We were just going over suspects in the Texas Highway patrolman's death," Katherine said with a nervous laugh. "You're going to think we're crazy."

He cocked his head to eye the list beneath Katherine's pen. "No. Maybe I can help. Who's on the list?"

* * *

Darlita played the message from Trent on her cell phone and quickly dialed a number.

"Hola."

"This is Darlita. I think he knows!"

"Your husband?"

"Si!"

CHAPTER FIFTEEN

Katherine sat at her computer in her nightgown the next morning. She was scanning the headlines of the *New York Times* when she heard a bustling noise on her back porch and the door open.

She gasped. Only Carmen had a key, and it wasn't her day to work.

"Ms. Bell?" Carmen called. "Ms. Bell!"

Katherine left her computer and rushed to meet her housekeeper. "Is something wrong, Carmen?"

"It's not right, it's just not right!" Carmen said.

"Carmen, calm down and tell me what you're talking about."

"I've been thinking about this," Carmen said. She inhaled and sobbed, casting her eyes down. "I have to talk to *somebody* about it!"

"Whatever it is, you can tell me," Katherine said quietly.

Several minutes passed before Carmen regained control enough to talk. "I left here early, you know. You said it was all right to leave and go over to my other job?"

"Yes, I remember. You needed to be at Sam Bassinger's house."

"Well, I decided to stop for some cleaning supplies first, and I ran into my cousin and her children. I haven't seen them in a long time ..."

Carmen wrung her hands as she spoke, and then she stopped, at a loss for words.

"Go on. What has happened to upset you?" Katherine prodded.

"Oh, Ms. Bell. I don't like to talk about people," she moaned.

"Carmen. What happened?"

"Well, I was late when I got to Mr. Sam's. I have a key, like I do to your house, and I let myself in his side door near the kitchen."

"Yes," Katherine encouraged.

"Oh, Ms. Bell, I heard *laughing*! A *woman* laughing, and it was coming from Mr. Sam's spare bedroom. And I heard him laughing too." Carmen raised her huge, brown eyes to meet Katherine's.

"And the woman, she came out into the hall where I was standing."

Carmen raised her hands and slapped the sides of her face, which held a look of horror. "Oh, Ms. Bell! She was naked!" She waved her hands in the air. "I was so *embarrassed*!"

Katherine tried to hide her surprise and stay calm. "Well, I can understand what a shock it must have been—to see anyone—in that—state."

Katherine noted the deep frown on Carmen's face and added, "But Sam Bassinger is single man, Carmen. And I'm sure he must entertain ladies."

"Yes!" Carmen covered her mouth with her hand and looked at Katherine with wide, fearful eyes. "But, Ms. Bell, the lady was *Ms. Johnson*, that dead patrolman's wife!"

Katherine gasped. "No."

"Should we do something, Ms. Bell? It is so wrong!"

"Let me think about this," Katherine said. She put her arm around Carmen's shoulders. "Why don't you go home and rest. I'll figure out what to do with this information."

Carmen's eyes widened with fear. "Yes, but *please*, don't get me in trouble. My husband, he has no papers!"

Katherine walked Carmen to the back porch and watched her leave by the side gate.

Katherine sat on the porch, assessing this new development. *Maybe this explains the strange cars in Sam's driveway during the day. Can this be related to the patrolman's murder? I need to call my brother.*

Bananas barked fitfully. Katherine glanced at the little dog who was braced on her hind legs guarding her territory as a feral cat lurked near the wide iron gate at the lower end of the walled yard.

Katherine heard a whirring sound and looked up to see a hummingbird looking for birdfeeders. She had not refilled them this late in the season.

Should I feed it? Maybe sugar water will strengthen it for migration.

She got up quickly and hurried to unhook the empty hummingbird feeder from a low, bare limb of the rain tree near the porch. As she carried it back to her porch, she saw Doris approaching the side gate.

"Yoo-hoo, Katherine!" Doris waved her new cane. "I saw you on my caller ID. I have Sandy with me. OK?"

* * *

Barrett went inside the small post office in Fort Davis to pick up his mail; Jane waited in the parked delivery truck. She watched him come out clutching a handful of envelopes; worry lines were engraved on his forehead.

"They say hard work won't kill you, but worry will," she mused out loud while wondering how they would ever meet the bills. She heard Barrett sigh deeply as he opened the door.

He doesn't know how we'll meet the mortgage!

She forced a smile as he slid behind the steering wheel. "Any good news?"

"I don't think so," he muttered and started the engine.

"Barrett, do you mind if we stop by Ms. Bell's house in Alpine?"

"Whatever for?"

She kept her eyes on the road ahead. "I think she could be a good customer for our produce. Maybe we could drop some samples off?"

"I doubt if anyone thinks of Ms. Bell as needy."

"Well, maybe we don't know what she needs."

Barrett's eyes turned soft. "You're a good woman, Jane."

She leaned into him and touched her lips to his cheek. "I know how desperate you are about the ranch ..." She stopped. They were both too on edge to discuss the mortgage payment.

They drove in silence. Once in Alpine, Barrett turned left onto Loop Road and drove up the mountainside. He slowed near the Bell house and pulled into the front driveway. The truck door creaked loudly as he opened and shut it. He stood looking toward the house.

Jane got out on her side and raised a flattened palm to shade her eyes as she looked at him. "Should we take her some cheese and eggs?"

"Sure. You bring 'em."

He met her behind the panel truck, opening the doors so she could get the products out of the back. Together they walked to Katherine's front gate. "I think you hafta go in this way to get to her front door," he said, unlatching the heavy wooden gate.

They climbed the front steps, and Jane took a deep breath and rang the doorbell. They heard a dog bark within.

"I think she's home," Jane whispered.

Katherine opened the front door with Bananas wedged in front, wagging her tail.

"Ms. Bell?" Jane began.

"Yes?"

"I'm Jane Compton, and this is my husband, Barrett."

"Barrett and Jane!" a voice yelped from inside the house.

Doris came up quickly behind Katherine saying, "Katherine, they're from Fort Davis." Doris smiled broadly at the couple and then at Katherine.

"Won't you come in?" Katherine welcomed.

"Thank you," Barrett said quietly and removed his hat.

Jane handed a carton of eggs and a package wrapped in brown grocery paper to Katherine. "We brought you some stuff from our place."

Katherine watched her blush as she stammered, "Just a little late welcome to the area. I bring fresh vegetables and cheeses into town each week to sell."

Katherine took the offerings. "Thank you. How very kind. Will you put me on your list as a customer? Please, come in. May I take your coats?"

"We can't stay," Barrett said.

Sandy stood as the couple entered the living room.

Katherine made introductions. "Barrett and Jane, this is Sandy Wisner. He's doing graduate work at Sul Ross."

Doris followed Katherine and the Comptons into the living room but spoke to Sandy. "Barrett and Jane are cattle ranchers in the Davis Mountains near Fort Davis."

The men shook hands.

"Do you have honeybees?" Sandy asked. "I've taken an interest in sustainable living in remote areas."

Barrett exchanged a look with his wife. "No," he answered slowly, "but it sounds like a good idea."

"Honeybees may be one of the most important elements to the human food chain," Sandy said. "They're essential in pollination of fruits, vegetables, flowers, and nuts—and they provide amazing economic benefits."

"May I get anyone something to drink?" Katherine interrupted.

The men were engrossed in conversation and didn't hear, so she turned to Doris and Jane. Each shook her head.

"Excuse me while I put these wonderful gifts in my refrigerator." Katherine hurried toward the kitchen. She returned quickly and saw the ladies standing near her back window talking and looking out across the yard.

Katherine crossed the room to join them, stealing a glance at the men sitting next to one another in serious conversation.

Doris looked at them too and chuckled. "They may not come up for air—or food."

"Have you had lunch?" Katherine looked from Doris to Jane. "I have a lasagna casserole that I can warm."

"Oh no, we couldn't." Jane shook her head and looked toward Barrett, who didn't notice. He was hanging on every word Sandy spoke.

"Thank you, Katherine, but Sandy is taking me to lunch today."

Katherine thought Doris looked pleased with her announcement.

"We were on our way and just popped by to see why you called."

"Oh," Katherine sighed. "I needed someone to talk to about the Frank Johnson murder."

At the mention of Frank's name, Barrett and Sandy looked at Katherine.

Katherine returned Barrett's gaze. "Did you know Frank?"

"Yeah," he said. "He was a friend."

Katherine moved to where the men sat in the living room, and the ladies followed.

"Could we talk about him?" Katherine entreated. "Do you know his wife—I mean his widow—Trudy?" Katherine sat on the opposite sofa facing the men, who both looked rigid and pale.

Barrett looked at Jane. She smiled and nodded back.

"I don't mean no disrespect, but Frank told me that him and Trudy was havin' problems." He paused and added, "He said he'd get to keep Pete when the facts was known."

Katherine glanced around the silent room. She knew that Trudy was having an affair, so she was prepared for this shocking information, but Doris looked stunned and Sandy, stricken.

After all, Sandy and Sam are first cousins.

She waited for Barrett to look up again so she could catch his eye. "Thank you, Barrett. This is important information. You were right in telling it. Captain Butler and Ranger Trent need to hear this too. Could you do that? Tell them as soon as possible?"

"Yes, ma'am." Barrett nodded. "If you think it'll help find Frank's killer."

Doris stood up clutching her walking cane. "I've lost my appetite." She looked at Sandy, who appeared ill. "Let's go have a drink at Zeppie's. Anybody game?"

After Katherine's guests were gone, she went to her phone and dialed her brother. After four rings, the ranger's answering service said, "Leave a message."

"Ambrose! It's Katherine. I need you to call me as soon as possible!"

She searched for a pad near the phone and dialed a number written there. "May I speak to Captain Butler, please?"

"I'm sorry, ma'am, but he's out of the office. Can someone else help you?"

"Out? Oh, no. I *really* need to talk to him!"

She felt a gnawing anxiety and wanted to talk to someone—someone in law enforcement.

"Well, could you tell me how I might reach Ranger Trent?"

"He and Sheriff Carlton went to Pecos today to pick up some prisoners, ma'am. Is there anyone else who can help you?"

"Oh, I don't know," Katherine said sullenly. "No, but thank you." She hung up.

Bananas waited at the back door to go out. Katherine moved toward her and asked, "What to do? Should I confront Trudy, or Sam?

"And say what? 'I know that you're having an affair?'"

"So?"

She opened the back door for Bananas to run out.

She went back to the phone to call Doris about it, but put the receiver down quickly, remembering that Doris wasn't home yet. She and Sandy were going for drinks.

She went to her burgundy chair and sat looking out the back windows.

Where was Butler?

It dawned on her that he might have gone to the Texas Panhandle to be with Susanna.

I have her number. Should I call and ask to speak with him?

No, definitely not at a time like this! She's burying her father.

Doris is spending most of her spare time with Sandy; Susanna is with her children in the Texas Panhandle ...

She heard Bananas's nails scraping the back door. She went to open the door to let her in.

"Oh, Bananas, if only Brann were here. *He'd* know what to do."

She walked back to the leather chair and sat.

If Brann were here, I would know what to do.

The many years of oneness with Brann had been fulfilling, but had they also robbed her of independent thought?

No, she decided. Shared decision making had strengthened and supported their partnership, and reduced their personal anxiety in crisis, especially during their daughter's manic episodes.

Marriage had provided intimate dialogue, and right now, she wished fervently for someone to counsel her on what action, if any, she should take.

She noticed Bananas hovering. *Had she sensed the anxiety?*

"Come on, little one; let's take a walk. It'll make us both feel better."

Bananas strutted alongside Katherine as they toured the inner walled yard. The recent freeze had taken its toll on the plants and trees. Pistachio trees had dropped their red and golden leaves, and the melting snow exposed gaunt, anorexic limbs. Buffalo grass had yellowed, roses waned, and the Maximillion daisies were dry on their stems.

She wandered across the yard to a weathered teak bench in the middle of her lavender bed and slumped onto it. Bananas continued investigating the premises.

A black-chinned hummingbird flitted among dry lavender stalks near Katherine.

Fragile beauty. Looking for security?

Was this what drew Trudy to Bassinger?

Security? Didn't she know what he was like?

She realized that her and Doris's "suspect list" wasn't adequate. Drug dealers were at the top of the list; they would certainly take the media box from the patrolman's car so they wouldn't be identified. Butler had told Susanna about that.

Illegals? No, they were desperate and running.

Kelly? She might be capable of shooting someone. She killed prairie dogs, according to Susanna. And she and Frank had been an item long ago. But why kill him now?

A lover? We only thought of Frank having a lover. Trudy has a lover! But, murder?

What are we overlooking?

* * *

Doris and Sandy sat in a dimly lit corner at Zeppie's. They raised freshly filled wine glasses and clinked them together.

"Hold all things lightly so that loss diminishes us not," Doris toasted.

Sandy hesitated, holding his glass in the air, and asked, "Did you feel diminished by the loss of your husband?"

"Oh, Sandy, no," she smiled and sipped the wine.

"And if you don't get the position as department head?" He kept his eyes steadily on hers, still holding the glass midair.

"Well, I'll be disappointed, but I will survive."

"Ah, survival. I know a little about that." He lifted his glass and drained it.

"Sandy, you seem troubled. Surely you know that this life and everything in it is but a shadow of that which is to come." She smiled and drank with gusto.

"Bullshit!" he exclaimed. "I know no such thing! That which I can see and touch and smell is the only reality."

Doris was startled. "And when age lessens that, then what?" she said in a calm voice. "Is reality gone?"

"I think I know what you're saying." He finished his wine and signaled the waitress for two more. "That I can only function in the here and now!"

"No, I'm not saying that. It's not about you, Sandy. But one can be strongly in the here and now while realizing that a greater reality exists," she said and emptied her glass.

There was silence.

"It's a joy to be with even one or two who know this too," Doris continued.

"Magnification?" His forehead held multiple creases in a tired face. He moved his elbows from the table as the waitress set two glasses of wine in front of them.

"But of course! And it could also be a way of escape." She raised her glass to clink his.

"Yes, escape. From hellfire and damnation! That's what life has been for me in this hick town!" His countenance darkened, and he gulped more wine.

"No. Not running from," Doris countered and leaned closer to him across the table, "but running to." The wine was bubbling in her brain. "To a place where we belong and have always belonged."

"Belong? A place where we *belong*?" Sandy drained his glass and pushed back, waving a hand to get the waitress's attention. He looked back at Doris. "Another?"

"Oh, no," she laughed and watched him raise one finger to the waitress. "I've had quite enough."

"Doris," he began.

She watched him fidget uncharacteristically in his chair, leaning back and then forward, putting his hands on the table and removing them. He looked so beautiful to her, but so unhappy.

"Is there something wrong, Sandy? Can I help?"

"Doris, I have something to tell you."

"Yes, Sandy," she smiled weakly.

"Doris, I'm, I'm utterly unavailable. I confess that I've been using our friendship as a cover."

The waitress brought more wine, and Doris heard Sandy thank her from a distance. His voice sounded like an echo as she left the room.

* * *

"Ambrose? It's Katherine again. It's two o'clock. I'm sorry to bother you at home, but this is urgent. Will you please call me when you get in?"

Where were people when you needed them?

The phone rang. She snatched it up quickly.

"This is Katherine Bell."

"Hello. Sam Bassinger here. I wanted to thank you for inviting me to your party last weekend."

"You're welcome."

"My pleasure. Ms. B, will you do me the honor of being my guest for dinner one evening this week?"

My God, he's a regular Blue Beard.

"Thank you, Sam, but I'm planning—" She thought of him being with Trudy. "Planning on doing something for that poor, young widow. You know? Frank Johnson's *wife*? She has a small child, and the two of them must be devastated!"

She covered her mouth to prevent a squeal.

"Of course," he responded quickly. "Very kind of you, Ms. Bell. Well, maybe another time?"

"Thank you, Sam. I look forward to talking to you again soon. Good-bye."

She shut her eyes tightly and banged the phone down.

* * *

The doors were locked, the lights were out, and Katherine climbed into bed. She decided that she might not need the sleeping pills she had been taking since Maureen's death—and then

250

Brann's. Sleepless nights invited that bogeyman—
memories.

She realized that some of her numbness
was gone; she actually cared about Doris and
Suzanne and what happened to them, and the
young patrolman. She even cared about the new
neighbors. Not that she cared about everything.
*I've heard when you care about everything, that's
sadness; and when you don't care about anything,
that's depression.* This felt like waking up out of
a long sleep.

She reached for a devotional book from her
bedside table that Doris had given her.

*Why didn't anecdotes ever note the silence of
broken hearts?*

She read and then dozed off with snores that
rivaled those of Bananas's at her feet.

The phone rang. Katherine felt the bed quake
as a startled Bananas jumped upright.

She leaned forward, the open book tumbling
from the bedcovers, and checked the bedside
clock: 10:30 PM.

She plucked the phone from its cradle. "Hello,"
she said hoarsely.

"Ms. Bell, sorry to call so late, but I just got in
and heard your message saying it was urgent,"
Captain Butler said. "Are you all right?"

"Yes," Katherine said. "Thank you for returning
my call."

She sat up in bed propped against her pillows and pulled the covers up to her waist.

"I've learned some important things today regarding Frank Johnson that I thought you ought to know." She began telling him what she had learned.

Katherine heard a "beep" on the line. It was the sound of call waiting, signaling that she had another incoming call.

"I'm sorry. Will you hold for one moment, Bill?"

She clicked to answer the second call.

It was her brother, Ambrose. She promised to call him right back with her news after the conversation with Butler.

CHAPTER SIXTEEN

Ranger Trent leaned back in one of Sheriff Carlton's swivel chairs, enjoying a cigar. He propped his size-thirteen stovepipe boots on the desk. Sheriff Carlton sat across from him in like fashion.

"The way I see it …" Trent paused, turned his nose to the ceiling, and blew a perfect smoke ring. "Sam Bassinger fell to fornicatin' with that patrolman's wife."

The desk phone rang. "Hellfire! Jest a minute, Ranger," Carlton muttered. He jerked his boots from the desk to the floor, reached over, and picked up the phone.

"Carlton here," he growled.

"The people you were expecting are here, Sheriff," a woman's voice said.

"OK. Ask 'em to wait. I'll come out and get 'em."

"Yes, sir."

He put the phone down. "Ms. Bell is here, and so are the others, jest like you asked."

The ranger nodded approval.

"Like I was saying." Trent clenched the cigar in his teeth, calm and composed. "The patrolman's wife tells Sam that her husband is on to 'em, and he plans to make everything public. Sam Bassinger has a lot to hide."

He winked and smirked at the sheriff, leaning forward to snuff the stub in a black plastic ashtray on the desktop. He lifted his boots, dropped them to the floor, and sat forward. He clamped his lips and nodded. "I think he did it!"

"What does your sister have to do with this?" asked Sheriff Carlton.

"She told me last night about what she'd heard. That's why we're here this mornin'." Arthritis slowed Trent's standing. He placed his hands at the small of his back, stretched his long torso upward, straightened, and adjusted the gun at his hip.

The sheriff waited and met the ranger's eye. "Ready?"

"Yep."

Sheriff Carlton opened his office door and sauntered past his secretary's desk to the waiting area.

Katherine could feel the tension in the room as the sheriff walked in and looked around. She wished that Doris and Susanna were here with her. And Bananas.

Maybe this was crazy!

Two chairs away from her, Trudy Johnson sat primly reading a fashion magazine. Barrett Compton sat on her left looking apprehensive. Sam Bassinger lounged casually on the opposite side of the room.

"OK, folks," the sheriff said, nodding to each person. "Ranger Trent and I'd like to see you, one at a time."

His eyes singled out Katherine. "Ms. Bell, would you come in, please?"

Katherine rose from her chair and followed the sheriff to his office. *I hope I haven't created a mess!*

"Mornin', Katherine." Trent greeted her with formality and pulled a chair from the long table for her.

"Ambrose." She smiled and then looked at Carlton. "Sheriff."

She sat in one of the chairs in front of the desk. The sheriff closed the door and took a seat behind his desk.

"Now, Katherine," Trent drawled. "Tell us again what you heard 'fore we bring those other folks in here."

* * *

"Bassinger and Compton, follow me," the sheriff called out in the waiting area.

The men traded looks, got up stiffly from their chairs, and followed the sheriff into the back office.

He closed the door behind them, saying, "OK, boys. Let's get some facts straight!"

Ranger Trent, standing tall to meet them, said, "Have a seat."

The two sat in swivel chairs near the barred windows. Katherine watched their faces as her brother confronted them. Each held a Western hat and looked uncomfortable.

"The sheriff here has your sworn statements about your whereabouts the night Highway Patrolman Frank Johnson was shot." Trent nodded toward the sheriff seated at his desk next to a recorder.

"Sheriff Carlton will tape-record this meeting. Is there anything either of you wish to change in your statements?"

Katherine thought Ambrose's demeanor intimidating. She had never seen her brother in a professional capacity. She watched Barrett lean forward eagerly and Sam ease slowly back in his chair.

"Can we smoke in here?" Sam asked, reaching in his shirt pocket.

"That can wait. Answer the question," Trent said.

"No, sir," Sam said, stretching back and sticking his legs and boots in front of him, crossing one over the other. "I told the truth, the whole truth, and nuthin' but the truth. Sir."

"Compton?"

Barrett answered softly as he leaned forward in his chair. "No, sir. I can't think of anything."

"Take your time now," the ranger said with emphasis. "Bassinger, you first. Tell me what you did that day."

"Well, that's been a while. Best I recall, I checked with Barrett that Wednesday mornin' and told him the plan was set up with Scrim and his partner to meet around three o'clock in the morning. Told Barrett," he looked at Compton, "to meet me at my warehouse in Marathon about nine o'clock that evening, and we'd go to a spot I'd picked out in the park. It's hard diggin', and I wanted to make sure we had plenty of time."

"That's the Big Bend National Park?" the sheriff asked, tilting his head toward the recorder.

"Right, sir."

He must surely be nervous, Katherine thought, watching Sam. But he didn't look it.

"Go on," Trent said, leaning on the edge of the desk.

"Well, he got there on time. Like I told you, we drove to the park in my pickup. We dug and loaded the plants I'd spotted earlier. We didn't take soil so we could stack 'em bare-rooted. Then we went to meet the eighteen-wheeler. They were waitin' on the highway outside of Marathon. We pulled over and loaded the plants onto their rig." Sam paused and twirled his hat in his hands. He looked at Barrett and then back at the ranger, "And then we left!"

"And then what did you do?" the ranger prompted.

"We drove back to my warehouse. Barrett got in his truck and drove away. I did the same. End of story."

The room was silent for a moment.

Trent turned to Sam's partner. "Is that right, Barrett?"

Barrett gave his full attention. "Yes, sir."

The ranger made some notes and then asked, "Compton, was there anyone at Sam's warehouse when you arrived that evening?"

"Yes, sir," Barrett answered. "But I don't know who. Sam was waitin' outside, and I jest got in his pickup and we went."

Katherine assessed both faces. They looked strained.

"Sam, who was at your warehouse?" the ranger asked but kept his eyes on the yellow pad where he was scribbling notes.

Sam didn't answer.

The ranger looked up and stared a hole through Sam. "I asked you a question. Who was at your warehouse?"

"A friend," he said in a low voice.

"Was this friend a man or a woman?" the ranger pursued.

Sam looked down and twirled his hat in his hands. "The latter, sir."

"Who was that woman, Sam?" The ranger's eyes never left Sam's face.

"I—I'd rather not say, sir," Sam stuttered.

"Had this woman been at your warehouse all day?"

"No, sir. Just 'fore Barrett got there, sir." Sam pulled his feet back near the chair and, for a moment, appeared nonchalant.

The ranger stood and walked around the desk, getting close to Sam's face. "For your information, you little piss ant, I'm sure I *know* who it was."

His tone frightened Katherine, and she thought Sam would fall from his chair, his face grew so pale.

"What I want to know is," the ranger's voice expanded in volume, "did anyone else come to your warehouse that night?"

"Yes, sir. But I didn't see them, sir. They came and went 'fore I got home to Alpine, 'fore dawn."

"Who were these people?" the ranger probed.

"It was Wednesday, sir. My uncle Harlan brings my cousin Sandy over on Wednesday nights for an AA meeting."

Sam was now past pretenses of nonchalance, Katherine realized, as she heard a tremor in his voice.

"Don't they both live in Alpine?" the ranger asked, standing in front of Sam. "Why would they drive to Marathon for an AA meeting?"

"Yes, sir. But my uncle doesn't want folks in Alpine to know that Sandy attends. Sandy is less known in Marathon. So, he drops him off and picks him up on Wednesday nights. And he waits at my warehouse 'til it's time to go. I have an office there."

"And what is that timeframe, Sam?" The ranger strolled over to sit on the desk again.

Sam was sitting erect now. "Well, sir, the meetings start about nine o'clock and can sometimes go 'til midnight or after."

"So where were you at nine o'clock?" Trent pursued.

"I was on my way to the park with Barrett." Sam stared at the tips of his boots as he crossed one leg over the other and then uncrossed them to sit forward in his chair.

"Compton." The ranger turned and watched the young rancher's eyes snap to attention. "What time did y'all return to Sam's warehouse?"

"About 4:00 AM, sir."

"Were any cars at Sam's when you returned for your truck?"

"No, sir." Barrett's voice was steady.

"Where did you go when you left Sam's warehouse?"

"I drove home to Fort Davis, sir."

"Can your wife verify that?"

"Yes, sir."

"Bassinger. Where were you the remainder of the night?"

"Back home in Alpine, sir."

"Can anyone verify that?"

"No, I was alone."

The ranger walked to the desk again and turned back to Barrett. "All right, you can go for now."

Sam and Barrett got to their feet and began to shuffle toward the door.

"Not you, Bassinger," Trent said firmly.

Sam did a double take and looked at the sheriff with his eyebrows arched and mouthed pursed. "What the hell?"

Trent glanced at Katherine and then at the sheriff. "Can somebody bring us some coffee?"

He pulled a cigar from his shirt pocket and began stripping the wrapper. "Do you mind if I smoke, Katherine?"

Katherine stood too. "Yes, I do mind because I have a reaction to smoke in a small room." Her brother's jaw dropped. "But I need to excuse myself to go to the ladies room. An open window might help?"

As she made her way to the door, Katherine saw the sheriff stop the recorder and heard Sam Bassinger say that he wanted his lawyer present. She heard the tape recorder click on again and looked back to see Sam pacing in front of the barred windows.

Katherine almost ran into the sheriff's secretary at the door. "Excuse me," they both said at the same time.

The woman stretched her head around, searching the room. "Sheriff!" she said nervously. "Ms. Johnson said that she wouldn't be questioned without a lawyer present."

The ranger pulled the cigar from his lips. "Did she leave?"

"Yes, sir. She's in quite a tizzy."

"What's that?" The ranger cupped his hand behind one ear.

"She's crying and carrying on." The secretary rolled her eyes.

The ranger exchanged a look with the sheriff, who asked, "What now?"

Trent tossed his head toward Sam. The sheriff caught his gesture and walked across the room.

"Sam Bassinger, you are under arrest on suspicion of murdering patrolman Frank Johnson. You have the right to remain silent ..."

* * *

Katherine, knowing that she might be tied up with Trent for an hour or so at the sheriff's office that morning, had placed a bowl of water on the back porch and left Bananas outside until she returned.

She arrived to greet an eager face and swishing tail at the back gate.

"Oh, a king's ransom for a friendly face! Bananas! I'm so glad to see you!"

She opened the gate and stooped to ruffle the little dog's fur and scratch behind her ears. Bananas leaned into Katherine.

"Have you been keeping intruders out of our yard? Like ferocious cats and birds?"

Katherine heard the phone ringing as she turned the key in her door lock. She rushed, catching it on the third ring, saying breathlessly, "This is Katherine Bell."

"Katherine. This is Darlita! I *need* to talk to you!"

"Hi, Darlita.

"Of course. When would you like to get together?"

"I'm nearby. Could I drive over now?"

Katherine was puzzled. "Is my brother coming too?"

"Oh no! Has he called you?" Darlita asked breathlessly.

"Not about visiting," Katherine responded. "Are you in trouble?"

"I'll be there in five minutes!" Darlita said and hung up the phone.

* * *

Katherine sat in her burgundy chair by the back windows. Darlita had come and gone.

So many secrets.

The phone rang, and she answered.

"Katherine, it's Susanna. We're back!"

"Oh, I'm glad you are! I can only hope things were OK for you?" she asked tentatively.

"Yes," Susanna answered. "The kids and I got to spend a little time with Dad before he passed. I would like to see you, Katherine, and talk to you about it."

Katherine glanced at her watch. "Can you meet me for lunch at noon?"

Susanna hesitated. "You mean now? At Sixth Street?"

"Right. Can you come?"

"Sure. See you there in a few minutes," Susanna said.

Katherine sat the phone back in its cradle, and it rang again.

She stood and grabbed it. "Hello!"

"It's Doris. What *happened*?"

"Sam Bassinger has been arrested for the patrolman's murder! Can you meet me for lunch right now, and I'll explain."

Doris gasped, "Sam?" Her breathing was audible and her tone anxious. "You want to meet *now*?"

"Right. Susanna's back home. We can all talk over lunch. Can you come?"

"Yes," Doris said. "I want to know *everything*!"

Katherine replaced the phone and looked down at Bananas. "OK, little girl. You can ride with me and wait in the car."

She snatched her purse and retrieved the dog leash from the closet and then met a gleeful Bananas at the back door.

Katherine drove downtown and parked across the street from the Sixth Street Café. She opened all of her car windows about half an inch to provide fresh air for Bananas, who lay on a warm sheepskin in the passenger seat.

"I'll be back soon," she told the puppy and poured bottled water into the plastic bowl on the floorboard. She got out and looked around. She didn't see Doris's yellow Bug, but she glimpsed Susanna entering the café.

Katherine checked her watch: 12:15. Where was Doris? She hurried into the café and joined Susanna at the glass pastry cases.

"Oh, *yes*! Key lime pie. And vegan oatmeal cookies!" Katherine's mouth watered as she spoke.

Susanna turned and gave Katherine an enthusiastic hug. She was about to speak when the bell jangled, and they both looked toward the door, expecting to see Doris. Instead, Alice Parsons flounced inside.

"I really need to get a cell phone," Katherine mumbled as she turned back to the display case.

"May I help you?" the owner asked.

"We're waiting for Doris Kemp, but I guess she's been delayed," Katherine began.

"Oh, I'm sorry, Ms. Bell. Doris called. She left a message for you that something important came up, and she would be a little late. She asked for you and Susanna to wait for her here if you could."

"Thank you, Barbara." Katherine felt relief.

"You're welcome. Do you want to order while you're waiting?"

"Let's order," Susanna said. "I have something to tell you."

"OK." Katherine turned back to the counter. "Yes, thank you, Barbara. I'd love a bowl of tomato-basil soup with your sourdough bread."

"I'll have the same," Susanna chimed.

Katherine began to open her purse.

"That's OK. Just pay when you leave." Barbara whisked clean white bowls to a steaming soup tureen. "Y'all have a seat, and I'll bring it out. Did you want something to drink?"

"Just water. We'll get it."

The ladies went to the drink bar where they clinked ice in their glasses and added water and wedges of lemon. They didn't hear the door open.

Doris's voice hissed from the door she held slightly open. "Katherine!"

Katherine's smile faded when she saw Doris's face—anxious and distorted. She rushed toward her. "What's wrong?"

"I need you both to meet me at my car," Doris whispered, twisting right and pointing her finger up the street to her yellow Volkswagen.

"Now?" Katherine asked.

"Now!" Doris turned and began walking briskly up the street.

Katherine sped back to tell Susanna and then to the counter where she tried to get Barbara's attention.

A young man came to help instead. "May I help you?"

"I'm sorry. I don't have time to explain. Tell Barbara that we'll be back later for our soup! My name is Katherine Bell." She hastened out the front door on Susanna's heels.

"Get in!" Doris said with urgency as she waited by the car. She pulled the driver's seat forward and motioned Katherine in back.

Susanna rushed around to the front passenger seat and hopped in.

"Bananas is in my car," Katherine protested, turning and looking through the back window.

The women's heads jerked and eyes widened as Doris pressed the gas pedal and went squealing forward into the street.

"Doris! What's going on?" Katherine demanded, trying to regain her balance.

Doris whisked left at the stoplight and headed up Holland Avenue. She whipped the car into the lot behind Zeppie's Bar. Katherine felt her insides lurch to and fro.

"We must hurry!" Doris said in a stage whisper as she killed the engine.

"What's this about?" Susanna protested.

"No time now! Meet me inside," Doris almost yelled as she fled to the bar.

Katherine and Susanna stared at one another and then hustled to catch up with Doris, who had disappeared inside the building.

It took a moment for Katherine's eyes to adjust to the darkness; her senses balked at the stale smell of cigarettes and beer. One side of the room was well lit and bustled with a lunch crowd seated at tables covered with red-checkered oilcloths.

"Over there," Susanna whispered, pointing beyond the bar to the quiet, dark recesses of the room.

Multicolored neon signs were scattered along the walls advertising beers and giving off eerie light as Katherine and Susanna passed a large jukebox with Patsy Kline sadly moaning, "I'm crazy for lovin' you."

They moved toward a table where Bill Butler stood tall, wearing his Stetson hat and a gun at his hip. He waved them over and an approaching waitress away.

"Ladies, please take a seat," he ordered.

"Bill?" Susanna managed with searching eyes.

He ignored her and motioned stonily at two empty seats on the opposite side of the long table. He took a seat next to Sandy Wisner, who was flanked by Doris.

No one spoke for what seemed like eons to Katherine.

"Doris told me that my cousin's been arrested," Sandy whispered. Only a slight waver in his voice gave away his calm demeanor.

Butler kept his eyes on Sandy.

Katherine exchanged looks with Susanna and twisted in her chair. She cupped a hand over her mouth and whispered, "For the murder of the highway patrolman."

Susanna's eyes bulged.

Sandy had hunched over the table, his eyes downcast. Silent.

"Sandy came to see me in my office a little while ago," Doris said quickly, turning to Katherine and

Susanna. She glanced back thoughtfully at the man next to her. "A few weeks ago he had been in the process of writing a paper for my criminal justice class. With his uncle being a judge, he chose to write about judges."

Doris looked again from Sandy to her friends across the table. Katherine nodded to Doris and looked back at Sandy, who had leaned forward with his head in his hands.

"Sandy diligently researched the Code of Judicial Conduct," Doris continued. "He read the eight canons for Judicial Ethics, followed by the list of what can lead to disciplinary action for judges.

"He learned that disciplinary action could be financial and could remove a judge from office and therefore from income."

Katherine felt bewildered and turned to see the same confused look on Susanna's face.

"I asked Captain Butler to meet us here when Sandy told me about the death of Frank Johnson," Doris continued. "Sandy said he would tell his story to compassionate people."

She turned to Sandy. "This is what you agreed to, Sandy." Doris gestured with her head toward the people at the table. "I think you should tell us in your own words."

Sandy silently lifted his hands and dragged spread fingers down each side of his face, closing his eyes. He took a deep breath, then another, and began. "I realized that my uncle was breaking all the rules."

He dropped his hands and opened his eyes, staring straight up at the ceiling. "I mean, 'uphold the integrity of office' and 'avoid impropriety and the appearance of impropriety,' for God's sake!"

He paused and dropped his head. "He's all I have. He supports me, putting me through college."

He stopped, closed his eyes, and leaned over, letting his forehead touch the table.

"Sandy," Butler encouraged. "Tell us what happened to Frank Johnson."

Katherine could hear Susanna draw a raspy breath.

Sandy stared unseeing. "It just happened," he said with a catch in his voice.

Silence.

"What happened?" Butler asked softly.

Silence.

"What did you do that Wednesday?"

"OK." He shuddered and sat upright. His voice was a low monotone. "Uncle Harlan takes me to Marathon for AA meetings each Wednesday night. I've just been a few times."

He wiped sweat from his forehead on his jacket sleeve and slowly pulled his feet from the floor and tucked them under his angular frame in the seat. He never met anyone's eyes.

"We drove over that evening." His voice began to clear and get stronger. "On the way, I told Uncle Harlan about my research paper. I knew that he had been meeting women at Sam's house in Alpine and at the warehouse in Marathon while I was at the meetings."

Katherine's eyes popped, and she tried to catch a look from Doris, who remained still with her eyes glued on Sandy.

"I asked him what would happen if he were found out." Sandy folded his arms across his chest and tucked his hands beneath his underarms. His eyes glazed, and he continued as if no one were there.

"He went bonkers! It wasn't Sam—it was my *uncle* who had been trysting with Trudy Johnson at Sam's house in Alpine for some time."

Katherine involuntarily wheezed. Sandy never noticed.

"He started yelling that if Frank Johnson took Trudy to court for a divorce, *he*'d lose *his* office as a judge, lose *his retirement*, and that *I* could expect to be out on the streets."

He hung his head and moaned, covering his eyes with the palm of one hand.

Doris placed her arm around his shoulders and gave a slight squeeze. Katherine and Susanna exchanged quick looks of amazement. "Trudy?" Susanna's eyes widened as she leaned into

Katherine. "The *judge* was having an affair with *Trudy*?"

Katherine nodded and kept her eyes on Sandy. Butler kept his demeanor in check, his eyes fastened on Sandy.

Sandy pulled from Doris's embrace and continued his story. "He dropped me at the meeting and said he'd pick me up when I called Sam's warehouse office. Ring once and hang up.

"The meeting was all about setting things right. It was long with a lot of personal stories, and they served some food afterward.

"I called Sam's number—ringing once and then hanging up—and in a few minutes I went out front, and Uncle Harlan came and picked me up."

He coughed.

"Here," Doris interrupted, pushing a full glass of water in front of him. Sandy clutched the glass and emptied it. He pushed the glass back to Doris without meeting her eyes.

"What happened on the way home?" Butler asked.

Sandy wiped his mouth with the back of his hand and sighed deeply. "Uncle Harlan said he was dog tired. Would I drive? I said sure. And when he got in the backseat, I checked the dashboard pocket for insurance papers in case we were stopped."

He paused and looked down. Suddenly the man looked like a child.

"What did you see?" Butler asked firmly.

"A gun. A Beretta." He drew his breath and released it with a gush.

Silence.

"Did you drive home?" Doris prompted.

"Yes. I drove home." He turned to Doris with eyes wide open, pupils dilated.

"Tell us what happened, Sandy," Doris urged gently.

His face hardened, like flint, as he told the rest. "Just outside of Marathon, I pulled over. Uncle Harlan was snoring in the back, so I knew it wouldn't matter if I slept too.

"I woke up a little later. I don't know how long I slept. Uncle Harlan was still sleeping, curled up in the backseat of his fancy sports car."

So it was Sandy *driving his uncle's car that night on the highway*, Katherine thought.

Sandy swept his eyes across the ceiling and threw his hands up. "He won't be able to keep that car. He's gonna lose everything. Me too!"

No one moved.

"I wanted to help somehow, fix things, do something to stop what was happening!"

Silence.

"What did you do next?" Butler encouraged.

"I started driving back toward Alpine and saw a big rig moving out ahead of us; it pulled out from the side of the road. Its taillights faded. When we got to where it pulled out, I saw a Texas Highway patrolman. He was standing in front of his car shining a light on a pad of paper. He was writin' on it. I slowed and saw it was Frank Johnson, Trudy's husband.

"I passed him slowly and made a U-turn back to where he was. I opened my window, stuck my head out, and said, 'Hey, I need to ask you about somethin'.'"

Everyone watched Sandy's face, and Katherine realized that he was thinking ahead to what happened.

"Did he know you?" Butler prompted.

Sandy's head jerked slightly as the question brought him back. "He recognized me. I stopped the car in front of him and reached in the car pocket and got Uncle Harlan's pistol. I don't know why I did that." He scrunched his shoulders upward, shaking his head. He looked down for a moment and up again.

"I got out real quick and walked up to him in front of the patrol car. When I looked at his face, I knew that no amount of words would change that man's mind. He was going to ruin it for everybody.

"I told him to turn around. He tried to talk to me, but I said, 'Turn around!' and when he did, I held the gun up to his head. I only meant to threaten him—I don't remember pulling the trigger—but I must have." Sandy choked as he sobbed, "The next thing I knew, he was laying face down on the ground!"

Everyone sat silent.

"Did you take his video box?" Butler asked in a low voice.

"The box?" He looked at Captain Butler. "No, Uncle Harlan did. He jumped up at the gunshot and came running. 'What have you done? What have you done?' he screamed at me! I was so confused! Then he pressed a button in his car and popped the trunk. He put on some gloves and got tools to pry the box out. Told me it'd look like drug runners did it, with the box missing."

His eyes dulled, and he sat still.

Butler, who had turned his chair toward Sandy to face him throughout the confession, placed a hand on Sandy's shoulder. "Are you ready to go in?"

No response.

Butler stood. "Sandy?"

Sandy gave a dazed look at Butler, who held his eyes. "Don't you think we should go to the sheriff's office? Your cousin Sam is in trouble there."

"Sam," Sandy moaned. He slowly got to his feet.

Katherine saw the sick look on Butler's face as he led Sandy away.

"What pathetic little creatures we are," she murmured to no one in particular. Then, remembering Bananas was waiting in her car, she urged Doris to leave.

CHAPTER SEVENTEEN

An hour before first light, Katherine stood wrapped in a long winter robe at her kitchen counter. She stirred cream into her first cup of coffee as Bananas nosily ate dry dog food from her bowl on the floor nearby.

Katherine picked up the kitchen phone and dialed Doris.

"Hello," Doris answered.

"Did I wake you?"

"Oh no." Doris yawned. "I'm getting ready for early classes."

"I'm having a few people over for supper on Friday. It's a birthday party for my brother. Darlita has been sneaking around to practice with some of her friends to do a skit called 'This is Your Life' to *surprise* Ambrose. It may be a little silly, but it's a big deal to her. Can you come?"

"Sure, I'll come. Alone again!"

Katherine could hear the hurt in Doris's voice. "Oh, Doris!" she sympathized. "When you get to be our age, the only available men seem to be drunks or philanderers, or they prefer other guys."

"Sad, but true. I was suspicious of Sandy's sexual preference, but why in the world did he have to lead me on?" Doris sighed.

"He's very complex, Doris. Sexual ambiguity is little understood—and rarely tolerated in cowboy country," Katherine offered.

"That's true," Doris agreed. "The pressure of guilt and paranoia must have been building over a lifetime. He obviously just snapped."

Silence.

"I heard that Trudy and her son are going to live with her parents," Katherine said.

More silence.

Katherine spoke again. "Have you heard from Barrett and Jane Compton?"

"That may be the one good thing to come out of this tragedy," Doris said. "Sandy suggested beekeeping to Barrett, and apparently he followed up on it. Jane told me they have enough honey business lined up to assure the payment of their mortgage."

"I'm so glad! They're good neighbors, good people."

Silence.

"Doris, are you all right?" Katherine asked gently.

Doris didn't answer right away, and when she did, her tone had changed completely.

"Well, all things considered, today I would say that on a happiness scale of one to ten, my life is at least an—eleven!" She paused dramatically. "I got the position I wanted at the university!"

Katherine squealed in unison with her friend. "Oh, Doris, that's wonderful!"

"It's a *milagro*, Katherine," Doris replied.

Katherine carried the wireless phone and her coffee to the study. She nestled in the burgundy leather chair by the windows overlooking her backyard.

Javier had stacked some firewood inside only yesterday, and Katherine had wasted no time in putting it to use. A newly built fire crackled in the fireplace across the open living room where Bananas now lay snoring in its warmth.

"I know you explained this, Doris, but I still don't understand how Captain Butler happened to be at Zeppie's with Sandy."

"Oh, right. We were all dazed at that time," Doris answered. "Sandy called me from Zeppie's just after you called for us to meet at noon. He was hysterical. When he mentioned 'killing someone,'

I told him to wait there for me. I was able to get Captain Butler on the phone, and he said he'd meet Sandy. I knew that you and Susanna were waiting … and Sandy, in his garbled call, said he needed compassionate witnesses."

"I got it," Katherine said. "Back to Trudy. She told the sheriff that she was *bored*. That staying home all day with a three-year-old and Frank working long shifts was *boring*."

"Only someone with no imagination gets bored," Doris stated. "Here's Trudy—limited resources but lots of time. It's a gift. Think of how creative one can be with time! Time to create good meals, gardens, watercolors, textile wonders. She could be doing photography, writing, learning a foreign language on tape. I could go on and on."

"You're preaching to the choir, Doris."

"Well, maybe our culture is experiencing too much instant gratification," Doris said. "Either that or living in fantasy worlds of books and movies."

On her soapbox, Katherine thought.

"People are losing the ability or the incentive to be creative!" Doris preached.

Katherine stared out her window as a brilliant pink orb lifted gloriously above Hancock Hill. "Not much 'instant gratification' in Far West Texas," she said as a slow smile lighted her eyes.

She sipped her coffee and focused on the beauty. "Unless you count the sunrise, the sunset, the smell of piñon ... Stranger than fiction, isn't it," Katherine declared.

"My promotion or Frank's murder?" Doris asked.

They both laughed.

"You've kept up with the proceedings," Katherine said. "Have Sandy and his uncle been formally charged?"

"Although killing a peace officer in Texas is a Capital offense punishable by death, the prosecutor has worked out a plea bargain in exchange for Sandy's testimony against Judge Bassinger, who could have been charged as a party to Capital murder," Doris answered. "And Bassinger voluntarily resigned rather than face the judicial committee. Can you believe? He didn't lose his retirement."

"Hmmm," Katherine groaned as Doris added, "It's not a perfect system."

There was a pause as both women reflected on recent events.

"And your neighbor, Sam?" Doris questioned.

"Doing a lot of growing up—I hope. Oh!" Katherine exclaimed. "Susanna e-mailed. She wants us to meet for lunch now that all the hullabaloo is past."

"I hope not today." Doris said.

"No, tomorrow. Can you make it?" Katherine asked, her eyes searching her side table for the TV remote.

"Sure. Here we go again," Doris answered. "See you at 12:30 tomorrow?"

"Right." As Katherine replaced the phone, she spied Susanna coming through the side gate. She glanced at the clock on her bookcase.

So early!

She jumped up and hurried to open the door. "Susanna! I'm glad to see you!" Katherine opened her arms for a hug.

"Thank you, Katherine. I never thanked you for the flowers you sent to my dad's funeral. It meant a lot to me."

"I wish I could've been there with you. Come in. Sit down," Katherine pointed to a comfortable chair near her burgundy one.

"That's OK. Everything happened so quickly," Susanna said as she sat down.

"You must be exhausted," Katherine said, noting the dark circles under Susanna's eyes. "I'm sorry we didn't get to talk last week."

Susanna shrugged and turned to the fireplace. "What a nice fire." She held her palms toward the glowing coals. "Yes, that was a long drive to the Texas Panhandle and back."

"Shall I take your coat?" Katherine asked.

"No, I can only stay a minute," Susanna said and put her hands in her lap.

"Well, sit right there, and I'll pour you a strong cup of coffee." Katherine hurried to the kitchen and poured coffee into a big cup. She added heavy cream and snatched two packets of raw sugar and a spoon.

"Here you are." Katherine set everything on the small table next to Susanna. "Would you like a scone with it? I can't resist buying them at Sixth Street."

"No, thank you. This is great." Susanna smiled and picked up the cup with both hands. "Sorry to come by so early. I'm on my way to Pioneer Plants."

"I'm happy you're here," Katherine said. "Is everything all right at the nursery?"

"Yes, thankfully. I've been cleared of any wrongdoing in buying plants from Sam since he presented falsified papers. I think he and his partner were given probation for a first-time offense. They're lucky not to go to prison."

"Ah, the Bassingers," Katherine said with a sigh.

"Yes," Susanna nodded. "Maybe Sam will finally grow up! Meanwhile, Leroy kept the business going for the few days I was away, and, good news! I have a prospective buyer."

"Oh?" Katherine did a double take at Susanna over the rim of her coffee cup, but Susanna remained silent.

Each sipped her coffee quietly and watched flames spark and sizzle in the fireplace. Bananas snored.

"I'm going to miss you, Katherine," Susanna said finally, warming her hands around the coffee cup. "You, and Doris."

"Why?" Katherine sat forward in her chair. "Where are you going?"

"The children and I will be moving to my dad's ranch in the Texas Panhandle over the Thanksgiving holiday weekend." She looked down at her coffee and up again with a wide grin. "And Bill is coming with us."

"Captain Butler?" Katherine asked, her eyebrows flying up.

Susanna nodded, and her face glowed. "He's just wonderful—to me, to the children. I never thought I could feel this way again, Katherine, but I have fallen head over heels in love with him. I just had to come tell you; he asked me to marry him!"

"Isn't this rather—" Katherine began. She didn't utter the word "quick" when she noticed pure joy radiating from Susanna's eyes. She considered how unbearably long the hours and days had seemed for her as a widow. She squeezed words over the emotions welling up inside her and smiled. "I'm so very happy for all of you. Will Bill get a transfer to Amarillo?"

"No. He's disillusioned with his role in preventing crime. And the work is all consuming." She took another sip of coffee and set the cup down, stating proudly, "He's going to help me run the cattle ranch."

She laughed at Katherine's expression and explained, "Daddy left everything to me. He and my mother lived there all their lives. It's a good place to raise kids." She wrinkled her nose. "Not that Lisa is happy about moving right now."

"How does she and Clay feel about Bill?"

"Now Lisa thinks he's *hot*." Susanna laughed. "Teenagers! But finally she's happy for me. Clay hangs around Bill constantly. He misses Marcos so much, and he seems to have transferred that longing to Bill." Susanna sat back in her chair smiling. "Bill has invited his daughter to come down this weekend to meet my kids and talk to her about our plans."

"This weekend?" Katherine clapped her hands. "I'm having a few people for supper. It's my brother's birthday, and his wife has secretly worked on a skit about Trent being a Texas Ranger. It should be fun for everyone, even Bill. Would it work out for you to bring your crew over on Friday? We'll announce your forthcoming marriage!"

"I'll have to check." Susanna sat forward and grinned. "Sounds fun, though. I could bring pumpkins for carving?"

"Yes! And why not bob for apples?" Katherine laughed. "We can make a little fun for everyone."

Susanna stood to leave. "Thank you for understanding, Katherine. I wanted you and Doris to be the first to know. Is she coming to lunch tomorrow?"

Katherine thought of Doris having good news too as she stood beside Susanna. "Yes, and I promise not to tell her your news. We'll just have lots of surprises."

She tightened the sash of her robe and walked Susanna out to her car.

As Susanna drove away, Katherine heard a distant, "Hello," and looked up the hill to see Ellie and Janis in gray sweat suits jogging toward her.

She raised her hand and waved.

The young women stopped near her, a little breathless.

"Janis," Katherine said pointedly to the young woman who reminded her so much of her daughter. "If you haven't found an art teacher, I would love to take you as a student."

Janis dropped her jaw. "You teach art?"

"Yes. I use to paint and teach, and this would help me begin again."

Janis reached out her arms. "Thank you."

Katherine returned the embrace. "No, it's you I thank for giving me a reason for tomorrow."